THE Secret Sisters CLUB

A GINNIE WEST ADVENTURE

Book One

MONIQUE BUCHEGER

Printed in the United States of America
Charleston, South Carolina
ISBN-978-1-939993-07-6

ISBN-978-1-939993-09-0

This book is dedicated to the many people who helped me weave my story. It would not have been the same without you.

Scoot, Pauline, Scott, N.B., Suzanne, Lance, Sheila, Debbie and Stephanie ... the Wests and I thank you for your diligence in helping me strengthen their story and present them in the most entertaining, heartwarming ways.

Mikey Brooks ... Thanks for bringing the Wests to life.

Hillary Straga ... For making the voices in my head come to life in the 'real' world.

Gracie ... Thanks for agreeing to pose as Ginnie on the covers. It means so much to me that you are willing to do this.

Jessie ... Thanks for agreeing to pose as Tillie on the covers. I love having the daughters of 'my boys' as the models.

Erin ... Thanks for the beautiful photos of Gracie and Jessie. All three of you did a fabulous job bringing Ginnie and Tille 'to life."

Anniqa, Daniel, Cassie, Ryan, Kristen, Andrew, Aeron, Brioni, Adam, Luisa, Ian, Aedric ... well, the last couple years have certainly been interesting. I want each of you to understand that there are no time limits on when your dreams can come true. I truly enjoyed being a mom before I remembered I also enjoyed writing. My new hobby wasn't always easy for you to accept, but so many times you stepped up to help me make my dream a reality. Thank you. May each of your dreams come true and may you each have many dreams to dream.

Violet... Welcome to the family. This has been an amazing year, my first grandchild and then my first books published. What can I say besides: Awesome sauce!

And to my husband, Kurt... your support has been sustaining and incredible and I love you even more than I did twenty-six years ago when we started our married journey together.

WEST FAMILY TREE

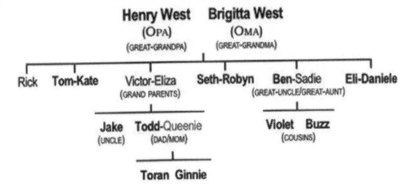

Henry West
(OPA)
(GREAT-GRANDPA)

Brigitta West
(OMA)
(GREAT-GRANDMA)

Rick   Tom-Kate   Victor-Eliza   Seth-Robyn   Ben-Sadie   Eli-Daniele
(GRAND PARENTS)   (GREAT-UNCLE/GREAT-AUNT)

Jake   **Todd**-Queenie
(UNCLE)   (DAD/MOM)

Violet   Buzz
(COUSINS)

Toran Ginnie

Bold denotes living family members

1

THE RACE

"Faster, Calliope!" Twelve-year-old Ginnie West tapped her heels into her horse's side. "They're gaining."

The thundering hooves grew louder. Ginnie peeked over her shoulder. Her best friend, Tillie Taylor, leaned forward, urging the black gelding to close the distance.

A field of ankle-high corn shoots lined the right side of the country lane. Knee-high alfalfa bordered the left. Each horse raced in one of the two gravel-and-dirt ruts formed by the family's assorted vehicles.

Ginnie glanced back again. Tillie's mount, Traxx, was only inches from Calliope's tail. The West family's red brick, two-story farmhouse grew smaller behind them.

Confidence welled inside Ginnie. She waved to her friend, certain she and Calliope would win this race. *How can we not?* Ginnie shifted in her saddle, the same one her mom had used when she rode Calliope's dam, Eternal Love. When Ginnie raced on horseback, she felt a kinship with Mama she never felt otherwise.

Facing forward, Ginnie grinned, feeling only a little guilty about Tillie's impending loss. The wind blew her blonde braids up and down behind her. She barely felt the light thumps of her ponytail holders on her back as she sped down the lane. Her body moved in perfect rhythm with her horse.

Ginnie lived for these moments lately. Off her horse, she could barely recall the mom she had lost eight-and-a-half years before in a tragic accident. But when she rode on horseback, she could be transported temporarily to the only memory she had of her mother, the two of them riding Eternal Love when Ginnie was three.

Ginnie's belly clenched with excitement and expectation. Just as she fully gave over herself to the joyful feeling of exhilaration in winning the race, a blur of silver-blue metal barreled toward them after turning from the main road. The car slid on the dirt, straight into Ginnie's path.

Heart thumping, Ginnie jerked Calliope to the right.

Traxx and Tillie broke left.

The car zoomed between them.

Brakes squealed. A horn blared. Tillie shrieked.

A second car, this one burgundy, followed the first car, blocking the rest of the lane and Ginnie's exit.

Without prompting, Calliope gathered herself and launched into the air, seeming to grow invisible wings. Ginnie was electrified. She loved the sensation of floating and the thrill of power that came when riding a jumping horse. Adrenaline fizzed through her like diet soda and Mentos as she and her horse sailed over the hood of the burgundy car.

Touching down near the end of the lane, Calliope crossed the main road in two leaps, narrowly missing a ragtop Camaro. A teenage boy in the convertible stood and punched a fist into the air.

"Awesome!" he yelled.

A woman, who must have been the boy's mother, threw Ginnie an angry look. "Sit down, Ryan!"

Ginnie beamed at the boy. Then she remembered Tillie's shriek. *Where is she?* Before she could find her, Calliope bucked, panicking Ginnie. "Hey girl, it's okay. You did good. Everyone's safe. Thanks for not letting the car hit us. You're okay." Ginnie stroked Calliope's neck as her mare snorted her frustration. "It's alright. We need to find Tillie."

Calliope settled as Ginnie wheeled her back toward the lane, watching for traffic to clear, her hand rubbing Calliope's neck as her eyes searched for her best friend.

Relief drowned the fizzing adrenaline when she spotted Tillie, still on Traxx, trotting by the row of mailboxes. Tillie urged him toward the blue car where her mom, Miss Amanda, stood, wiping her eyes.

After waiting for the traffic to clear, Ginnie walked Calliope across the road, all the while talking softly, trying to reassure Calliope as they neared Tillie and Traxx.

Tillie slid off the gelding and handed his reins to Ginnie.

"Are yeh ukay?" asked Mrs. MacGregor, in a thick Scottish accent as she got out of the burgundy car. "What did yeh think yeh were doing?" Their longtime egg-and-goat-milk customer waved her hands furiously, reminding Ginnie of a whacked-out windmill.

"I'm fine, Mrs. MacGregor." Ginnie's eyes widened at the woman's fury. "Sorry for the trouble."

"That's all yeh have to say? Sorry?" Mrs. MacGregor wagged an angry finger. "You coulda killed somebody with yer lunatic horse."

"It wasn't just Ginnie's fault," Tillie called behind her, while running to her mother. "Are you okay, Mom?"

Miss Amanda hugged Tillie. "You're not hurt, Ginnie?"

"We're fine." Ginnie stroked Calliope's neck.

Miss Amanda squeezed Ginnie's shin and then patted Calliope. "I can't believe I didn't see you until this far down the lane. I was reaching for a tissue, and you two just popped up out of nowhere. I'm so sorry! I could have killed you."

"Don't feel bad." Ginnie slid off her horse and stood next to Miss Amanda. "It's my fault."

Tillie's mom enveloped Ginnie in a hug, tugging the reins in her hurry. Calliope snorted her disapproval at being jerked.

"Yer father will be hearing about this, young lady," an angry Scottish-accented voice fumed.

Ginnie turned to Mrs. MacGregor, who glared at her. She caught movement behind the cranky older lady in the forms of her dad and twin brother.

"What happened?" called Ginnie's brother, Toran, as he ran toward them. Dad was just behind him.

"What are yeh going to do about this, Todd West? That girl of yers caused a five-car pileup and nearly gave me a heart-attack!" Mrs. MacGregor motioned impatiently to the now empty main road.

"I did not!" Ginnie shook her head and swung into the saddle. "No cars hit anybody or anything." She held the saddle horn, willing herself to calm.

"Yeh did, too."

Dad sucked in a breath. "Are *you* hurt, Mrs. MacGregor?"

"Don't blame the girls, Todd." Miss Amanda walked over to Dad and touched his elbow. "Ginnie's right. Nobody crashed. And this was *my* fault."

"Not so." Mrs. MacGregor pointed at Ginnie. "*That one* caused the ruckus."

"Mrs. MacGregor, *please*." Miss Amanda lowered her head. "I was in a hurry to talk to ..." Her voice caught. She blinked rapidly when she looked at Tillie. "Never mind."

"It's okay." Dad slipped an arm around Miss Amanda's shoulder. "Everyone's fine. Don't worry."

Tillie stepped closer to her mom. "We *are* fine."

"Nonsense! I, for one, am *not* fine. *That one* is a problem." Mrs. MacGregor wagged her finger angrily at Ginnie again. "Leaping over meh car, like a looney bird. I have half-a-mind to buy meh eggs at the Hansen place. And meh goat milk, too."

Ginnie choked out a half-hearted apology, in hopes her dad wouldn't believe the salt-and-pepper-haired lady's tale. "I'm sorry we scared you, Mrs. MacGregor."

After standing straighter, Mrs. MacGregor offered a curt nod and a tsk. "Well, I suppose it wouldn't be fair for yer Uncle Ben to lose a loyal customer over yer shenanigans."

"No ma'am," Dad and Ginnie answered together.

The older lady smiled triumphantly. "All right then. Amanda, please move your car and I'll conduct my business with Ben."

Tillie hid a giggle.

Ginnie whirled away and snickered. She and Tillie often teased each other about Mrs. MacGregor's crush on Ginnie's great-uncle, one her Uncle Ben did *not* return. It always amazed Ginnie that Uncle Ben could just 'smile and nod' and keep Mrs. Macgregor happy.

"Yes'm." Dad brightened his smile. "I'm sure he has a quart of milk with your name on it.

Corralling an 'oh brother' before it could escape her lips, Ginnie wheeled Calliope toward the farmhouse. Before they got too far she heard Dad's panicked voice yell, "Amanda!"

Ginnie turned in time to see Miss Amanda stumble into Dad's arms. He waved Ginnie down the lane. "Get some ice water."

A sick feeling swept over Ginnie. Forcing her eyes from Miss Amanda's crumpled body; Ginnie tapped her heels into Calliope's sides and rushed down the lane.

2

AN ODD LOOK

*G*innie slid out of the saddle, tied Calliope's reins around the old iron horse-head hitching post next to the farmhouse, and dashed up the four concrete stairs onto the porch, before rushing to the back of the farmhouse. Her great-uncle slid off the kitchen stool, where he was sorting eggs into various sized cartons, and towered above her. "What's wrong?"

"Tillie and I almost ran into Miss Amanda's car with the horses when she turned down the lane." Ginnie panted while snatching an ice tray from the freezer. She pulled a glass out of the cupboard.

Uncle Ben's blue-gray eyes widened. "Did anybody get hurt?"

"No, sir, but Mrs. MacGregor was there. She wasn't hurt, but she's kinda mad. She wants to talk to you."

"I'm sure *she* has a lot to say." Uncle Ben hurried toward the front of the farmhouse.

Ginnie filled the glass and followed him out the front door. She took the water to her dad, who was helping Miss Amanda out of the passenger side of her car. "How is she?"

"She's okay." He handed Tillie's mom the water. "Amanda, sip slowly.

Tillie twirled her long brown hair quickly around her finger. "M-Mom? You okay?"

"She'll be fine." Dad hugged Tillie. "She's just had a scare." Tillie nodded, twirling slower.

Dad locked his eyes on Ginnie's. "Put Calliope up. There's been enough racing for today... and stable Traxx here for now. You guys can return him to Austin later."

"Yes, sir."

"Come on in. Dinner's about ready." Dad offered Miss Amanda his arm. "Uncle Ben had planned to invite you before all the drama." She took it and let Dad lead her to the porch.

Ginnie searched for her great-uncle while walking toward Toran, who held both horses' reins. Uncle Ben stood next to the burgundy car. The anger in Mrs. MacGregor's face softened until she giggled like a silly girl with a crush on some boy at school, only the boy was Uncle Ben.

Ginnie laughed, then turned to her brother. "Toran, what happened with Miss Amanda?"

"She stumbled." Toran offered Ginnie Calliope's reins. "And Dad caught her."

Ginnie whistled. "I guess seeing two horses coming straight at you would freak anybody out."

Her twin shook his head. "Something else was wrong with her. She'd been crying—before that. Her eyes were red."

Toran's observations never ceased to amaze her. Toran didn't talk much, but his brain worked constantly, watching and analyzing the world around him.

Uncle Ben gave Mrs. MacGregor free eggs and milk as compensation for her worry. She left, promising to return soon. Ginnie rolled her eyes at the news and walked with Tillie to the family room at the back of the farmhouse.

"Wouldn't it be awful if Uncle Ben actually fell in love with Mrs.

MacGregor?" Tillie said with a grimace and then plucked a jelly bean from the candy dish. She sat on the dark plum couch. "What if he married her?"

Ginnie dropped next to her and sank into the cool leather cushion, shuddering at the thought. "Ewww!" She mimicked Mrs. MacGregor's accent. "Meh new name would be 'that one' and I'd have to move into the barn."

Tillie giggled. "Thankfully, she wouldn't be your step-mom, just your dad's. Or technically his step-aunt. Or does it matter?"

Ginnie shrugged and reached for a jelly bean.

Tillie tapped her cheek. "Or is anybody Uncle Ben married to just your dad's aunt no matter what? Since Uncle Ben is your grandpa's brother?" Tillie snitched another jelly bean and shook her head. "Yikes, your family tree sure is complicated."

"Oh, it matters. Uncle Ben and Aunt Sadie raised Daddy and Uncle Jake when Grandpa and Grandma died. Anybody else would just be Uncle Ben's wife." Ginnie shook her head. "But I don't see him getting married again. I don't even remember Aunt Sadie, but she's here." Ginnie nodded to the surrounding walls.

"Violets were her favorite flower, purple her favorite color, and goats her favorite animal, though I can't imagine why, ornery things." Ginnie wrinkled her nose.

Throughout the entire farmhouse goats, violets, or shades of purple could be found perched, draped, decorated, painted, or needle worked on pillows, paintings, pots, and portraits. Plates, assorted tins, and wooden plaques tole-painted with images of goats, and/or violets, hung on the walls.

Whenever Ginnie discovered a new goat or violet-themed decoration, she always thought it was Aunt Sadie's way of saying she still looked out for the family. Sometimes she wished her own mother had left such treasures behind, but the farmhouse had been Aunt Sadie's home, not Mama's. If Mama had anything like that, Ginnie had no idea where it would be.

"I wonder why she liked goats and violets. That seems like a strange combination," Tillie mused.

Ginnie shrugged. "I think she started collecting violets after Vi was born. But I'm not sure why she liked goats, especially Gertrude. She's just mean."

Recalling the last time she milked Uncle Ben's goat, Ginnie scowled. Gertrude had stepped on her foot and kicked the bucket over. On purpose, Ginnie was sure of it. "I wish Uncle Ben would get rid of Gertrude." Ginnie giggled and then lowered her voice. "Then Mrs. MacGregor would have one less reason to come over."

Dad entered the room from the kitchen, laughing. "She's here to stay. At least until Uncle Ben gets tired of her, and I don't see that happening any time soon."

Ginnie turned toward him and teased. "Are you talking about Mrs. MacGregor or Gertrude now?"

"Very funny." He tweaked her nose. "By the way, from now on, you guys can only race from the road to the farmhouse, understood?"

"Are we in trouble?"

"No." He rubbed a gentle thumb on Ginnie's cheek. "I nearly had a heart attack, and poor Amanda's pretty shook up. How's about you two set the table for dinner?" He waited for a nod and then went into the kitchen.

Tillie whispered to Ginnie. "Your dad doesn't have a girlfriend. He should date."

Ginnie laughed. "Are you kidding? *Who* would he date? He only goes to work, home, and church."

An odd look swept Tillie's face. She jumped to her feet. "Never mind! Let's set the table."

She marched off without a backward glance, leaving Ginnie to wonder: *What's up with her?*

3

"I DON'T DO CRAZY STUNTS"

*M*iss Amanda still seemed tense after dinner. When Uncle Ben stood, she asked to speak to him in the study. Then she looked at Tillie. "I'll just be a minute, so don't go far."

Tillie nodded. "Sure, Mom."

"We have to take Traxx back before dark," Toran said.

Dad looked like he wanted to say 'no', but gave a slow nod. "Be careful."

"Of course." Ginnie willed herself not to roll her eyes at her dad's overprotectiveness. She tapped Tillie's hand. "Walk with us to get the horses."

Tillie followed them out the door, hanging back.

"Why're you mad?" Ginnie asked.

"I'm not." Tillie glanced shyly toward Toran.

"Oh." Ginnie nodded her understanding. "Good. Let's swim in the creek tomorrow. It's been so hot."

"Good idea, my swimsuit's still here from last time."

"I think half your stuff is already here." Toran grinned at Tillie and unlocked Traxx's stall. "You practically live here."

Tillie's mouth dropped open. "I can't help it if Mom works."

"I didn't mean that as a bad thing." Toran arched his eyebrows at

Ginnie and then chuckled. "You're like a sister who actually knows how to behave. You keep Ginnie out of trouble and that keeps the peace."

"Hey!" Ginnie protested.

Tillie giggled. She smiled, but didn't quite meet Toran's gaze.

Toran returned her smile and reached for Traxx's halter. "Let's get you home, boy."

Ginnie saddled her horse and caught up to them outside the barn. She fastened her riding helmet, mounted Calliope, handed Tillie the extra helmet, then offered Tillie a hand up. "We can ride around here 'til your mom is ready to go."

"Cool." Tillie snapped her helmet on, stepped on a hay bale, and jumped up behind Ginnie. She wrapped her arms around Ginnie's waist. "If we were sisters, maybe Mom would buy me my own horse and we could race all the time. I might even beat you once in a while."

"Maybe, but Calliope likes to win."

"And you don't?" Tillie teased. She pointed at the porch and gave a low whistle. "Uncle Jake's looking sweet."

Dad's older brother tipped his black Stetson to them while he danced a jazzy box step down the front porch stairs, his shiny black cowboy boots tapping a quick melody on the concrete sidewalk that stopped in front of Dad's car. His boots crunched on the gravel as he neared the horses.

Toran whistled. "Let me guess. You're going out with Miss Clarissa —again."

Uncle Jake did a quick two-step, spun around, and grinned. "What was your first clue?"

"That goofy smile." Ginnie tapped her finger against her chin, appraising his green dress shirt and new black slacks. "But you clean up pretty good."

"You're hilarious." Uncle Jake tugged her platinum blond braid. "Stay put while I back out, Trouble. No time for the emergency room today."

Ginnie grinned. "Yes, sir."

"Them are fightin' words, young lady."

"Yeah, yeah." She rolled her eyes. "It's not like you don't say them."

"That's different and you know it." Uncle Jake reached up and pushed Ginnie's riding helmet further down her head and laughed. "I'm off to entertain a sweet young thing and don't need no smart-aleck kid harshing my mellow."

She saluted him. "Yes, sir. Won't happen again, *sir*."

Toran and Tillie laughed.

In one fluid movement, Uncle Jake snatched Ginnie off Calliope, hoisted her over his shoulder, slid her down his back head first so she looked at his new boots, up-close and personal.

"Hey!" Ginnie protested.

"Hay is for horses, straw is free, buy a farm and get all three." Uncle Jake dangled her like a fishing bobber, too close to the dirt road for comfort. "Are you done?"

"Yes. Geez." She tried squirming free of his grip, but couldn't.

"Good." With a quick flip, he stood her on her feet. "That'll learn ya to mess with me."

She grinned. "This ain't over."

"Bring it on." He winked at Tillie, put two fingers up for the 'victory' sign, and strode over to his tricked-out truck. Uncle Jake opened the door, stepped up on the gleaming silver running boards, and disappeared into the shiny black cab.

Toran chuckled. "Way to show him, Gin."

Ginnie glared, motioned Tillie to move into the saddle, stepped onto a flower planter made from an old barrel and then swung up behind her, adjusting behind the saddle. She wrapped her arms around Tillie's waist. They waited for Uncle Jake to back out before following him to the lane. He honked the horn to the tune of the *Army Cavalry Charge* and sped away.

Tires spat gravel in his dusty wake.

Ginnie looked at Tillie and groaned. "If you were my sister, Uncle Jake would think he could treat you like he does me."

Tillie giggled. "Well, I'm smart enough not to 'sir' him. He's a little nuts about that."

"Ya think?" Ginnie rolled her eyes and turned to Toran. "Let's race once more before Tillie goes home."

"Can't." Toran pointed at the front porch. "There's Miss Amanda. Tillie has to go."

Ginnie leaned back to give Tillie room to dismount. "It was fun today. See you tomorrow."

"Yeah. See you in the morning." Tillie swung her leg over Calliope's neck, slipped off the saddle, and landed on her feet. She unfastened the helmet and set it on the planter. "Will you put this away for me, please?"

"Sure." Ginnie moved into the saddle.

Toran and Ginnie waved and then waited for Miss Amanda to back out of her parking spot and drive down the lane before they followed. Ginnie grinned at her twin. "Hey, guess what?"

"What?"

"Calliope and I flew over the hood of Mrs. MacGregor's car. How cool is that?"

Toran pulled on Traxx's reins, stopping immediately. "That is *not* cool. You could've been hurt."

Ginnie rolled her eyes again. "Geez, you sound like Dad."

"You know you're not supposed to trick ride on Calliope."

"*I* didn't trick ride at all. Calliope did it all by herself. And since we're fine, quit sounding like an old lady, even Oma would think it was cool."

"Oma? As in Uncle Ben's mom? Are you delusional? She'd *definitely* tell you to keep all four hooves on the ground." Toran shook his head. "And don't change the subject."

"How did we ever get paired as twins?" Ginnie shook her head and then smirked. "Oh, I know, it must have been 'Opposite Day' in Heaven."

"More like, 'Be Your Sister's Keeper Day.'" Toran frowned. "Just because Mama did crazy stunts doesn't mean *you* should. I don't want to lose you, too."

"I *don't* do crazy stunts, but I *do* want to be like Mama." Ginnie gripped the saddle horn, trying to calm herself. "And I remember her best when I ride Calliope ... when I don't, Mama disappears."

"You can ride Calliope without jumping over cars." Toran kicked Traxx gently into motion, only stopping when they reached the end of the lane.

Ginnie sidled Calliope next to Traxx. Toran looked past her, lowering his voice. "I remember riding with her, too. But if she wasn't so in love with her horse, she'd still be here. *With us.*"

Ginnie swallowed her frustration, tired of explaining why she needed to ride. No reason would ever be good enough for her brother ... or her dad. She just needed to ride ... to remember her mother ... to be herself. *Why was that so hard for people to understand?*

4

TILLIE'S WISH

*T*illie sat in the front seat of her mom's silver-blue sedan, staring out the windshield, barely aware of the maple trees flying by.

I can't believe Ginnie didn't think about her dad dating Mom. We've talked about being sisters a million times. Why can't we be sisters for real? Her mom's dead and Jasper's ... well ... Jasper's gone. Thank goodness.

Jasper was Tillie's father. The nicest thing he ever did was leave almost six years ago. Tillie glanced at her mom's hair blowing in the breeze from the open window. *I wish she'd given me her auburn curls instead of getting Jasper's icky mouse-brown, stick-straight hair. But we both have blue eyes, so at least Ginnie and I look a little like sisters.*

"What's wrong? You're awfully quiet."

"Nothing." Tillie faced the passenger window, her cheeks warming.

A few days before her sixth birthday, Jasper had disappeared for good. Back then, Tillie still missed him.

Not anymore. Jasper left. Tillie moved on and found a new dad. Ginnie's dad. She called him DT—but only in her mind. DT stood for Daddy Todd. She told Ginnie everything, *except* about her secret dream to be adopted by DT That was her very own secret.

Tillie recalled the time she and Ginnie had been playing at the farm and Tillie had skinned her knee. Ginnie's dad had picked her up and rocked her on the front porch swing. DT had been kind. Tillie had believed him when he told her that everything would be fine. He said she was a special girl and that it was okay to cry.

With Jasper, it was *never* okay to cry. It was only okay to be invisible.

Mom turned into their parking spot and stopped. "Well?"

Tillie shrugged and forced a smile to her lips. "Just thinking."

"About what?"

"Nothing." Tillie mustered her most innocent look and changed the subject. "Mom, do you think I could have a horse?"

Mom smiled. "Where would we put it? We only have two bedrooms."

"Very funny." Tillie threw her mom a cheesy grin. "I bet Uncle Ben would let me stable it with Calliope. They have lots of stalls." Tillie opened her door.

Mom got out and shut hers. "I'm sure he would, but I can't afford to buy a horse *and* feed it." She straightened her shoulders and smiled too brightly. "Let's make some brownies."

Tillie followed Mom to the stairwell by their apartment. "Calliope grazes a lot. So would my horse. Grass is free."

"I know. But we'd still have to buy hay and oats." Mom hugged her. "I wanted a horse when I was your age, but I didn't even have a friend with one. Think of something more reasonable and I'll see what I can do for your birthday."

"Sure." Tillie walked to the kitchen. She knew asking for a horse was a long shot, but it also kept her mind off Jasper.

In the kitchen, Tillie got out some eggs, oil, and brownie mix and started adding the ingredients. She carried the bowl to the table to and sat next to Mom.

"Any thoughts for your birthday, honey?"

Tillie stirred the brownie mix. "Maybe a trip to the mall for a new outfit? Or the movies?"

Mom set her pencil down and looked Tillie in the eye. "You're going to be twelve. That's special. How about a party at Quincy's Pizza Palace?"

"Mom, *babies* go there for parties." Tillie squelched the urge to roll her eyes. "A new outfit and spending the day with Ginnie is fine. We can do lunch and get chocolate cheesecake."

"You're always with Ginnie." Mom patted her hand. "Of course we'll include her, but what about a *real* party, with other kids too?"

"Fine, we'll invite Toran and Austin."

Mom sighed. "Tillie, there *is* life outside the farm. Broaden your horizon a little. Let's invite your friends from school as well." Mom picked up the pencil. "We can send the boys home after games, cake, and pizza. And have the girls spend the night and do hair and makeup. We can rent a fun movie and make banana splits."

The thought of having a bunch of girls over made Tillie queasy. "I don't need a big party. I like hanging out with just Ginnie and Toran... and Austin. Uncle Jake calls us the Four Musketeers for a reason. We don't need anybody else."

"Matilda Grace, I know you don't like people to fuss over you, but it's your birthday. I want to celebrate you with your friends."

Tillie groaned. "Mom, I don't want a big party. Just take Ginnie and me shopping. Please? That's good enough."

She shook her head. "What twelve year-old doesn't want a real party?"

The kind of twelve-year-old who likes being invisible so people don't ask you questions you don't want to answer. Tillie smiled. "Mom, it's *my* birthday. I like being with the Four Musketeers. *I* think that would be fun."

I want you to marry Ginnie's dad—that's what I really wish for my birthday, Ginnie and I have talked about being sisters a million times. That's what I want ... to be sisters, only for real.

5

THUNDER AND LIGHTNING

A clap of thunder rattled the window. Tillie sat up straight in her bed. Her room lit for a brief moment like the strobe light at the skating rink. A second clap of thunder followed.

She snatched her pillow to her chest and hugged it tight. *It's just a storm. Nothing to freak out about.*

Tillie slid off her bed and headed toward the door. She willed her heartbeat to slow while searching the darkened room for Ginnie. Disappointment flooded her as surely as the rain splashing against the window cascaded down the pane. Ginnie loved storms and told Tillie crazy stories to calm her when they were together when thunder and lightning raged outside.

One time Ginnie had suggested wishing on lightning like they would on falling stars. They wished for ice cream and Uncle Jake had actually offered them some. *Another reason we should be sisters, Ginnie makes me feel brave.*

The last time Tillie had got caught in a downpour at the farm, she had paced. Toran explained that moist warm air collides with cooler air and forms rain. He kept Tillie busy teaching her about the four types of thunderstorms and explained what conditions needed to be met for each to exist. He never once made her feel stupid and his explanations calmed her fears.

That was one of many cool things about Toran. As long as he understood *how* things worked, he didn't spend much time stressing about *why* they did. He certainly didn't assign random motivations to inanimate objects like Tillie did. To Toran, a storm was just a storm, created because the atmospheric conditions were right. It wasn't a punishment for doing something wrong.

A brownie will make me feel better.

Tillie tossed her pillow to her bed and opened the door. She passed Mom's door and stopped. A strange noise came from the room. It sounded like a sob. She poked her head in the room as Mom reached for a tissue.

"Oh!" Mom slammed a blue leather-bound book closed. "Tillie, you scared me."

"I didn't mean too. I heard you crying." Tillie rushed to her bed. "What's wrong?"

Mom shook her head. "Nothing. I'm fine. Go back to bed."

"You're *not* fine. Why're you crying?"

"Because I'm being silly." Mom's eyes begged her not to argue. "Please go to bed."

Tillie searched her mom's face, debating whether she would obey or not.

Mom turned away and blew her nose. She pulled a fresh tissue from the pink box and dabbed her eyes. "I watched a sad movie and I'm being silly. Quit worrying. I'm fine."

No, you're not. Tillie gave a slow nod. She was tempted to ask the name of the movie, but didn't want to catch her mom in a lie. She leaned in for a hug. "Want a brownie?"

"Sure. Maybe with some milk?"

"Okay." She left her mom's room. When she returned, the blue book had disappeared. In its place was a well-worn novel. The box of tissues sat underneath the peach lamp. "Thanks, Tils, this will go perfectly with *Pull of the Yew Tree*." Mom took a sip of milk and set her glass on the nightstand. "You're a doll."

Tillie crawled up next to her mom and hugged her, throwing Mom her most insistent smile. "I know. But I still want to know why you are crying."

Mom returned the hug, scolding in her 'I'm not really mad, but please do as I say' voice. "Matilda Grace, I already told you why." She bent and touched their foreheads together. "It's my job to take care of *you*, not the other way around. Let *me* be the parent."

"Okay, Mom, whatever you say." A flash of lightning lit up the room. Tillie snuggled against her mom and closed her eyes.

But I have a back-up plan. I wish I may, I wish I might, have the wish I wish tonight: Please help Mom and DT get together so Ginnie and I can be sisters ... for REAL.

6

THE SCHEMING BEGINS

The hen house door squeaked open, letting in the morning sun.

Ginnie blinked at the brightness.

A familiar form filled the small doorway. She grinned at her best friend. "Hi, Tillie."

"Hey, your dad and Uncle Jake aren't home, right?" Tillie spoke so fast her words slid into one another.

"Yeah."

"Perfect."

"For what?"

"My plan."

Ginnie put an egg in her basket. "What plan?"

"The plan to make us sisters." Tillie squatted next to her and picked up two eggs. "For real."

Ginnie leaned back on her heels and smiled. "What are you talking about?"

"My mom, your dad. Let's get them together." Tillie added the eggs to Ginnie's basket. "They get married and we can have a slumber party every night. How cool would that be?"

"Very cool." Ginnie picked up another egg. "But I don't think my dad knows *how* to date."

Tillie rolled her eyes. "He must know *something*. He married your mom, didn't he?"

"When dinosaurs roamed the earth."

Tillie groaned. "Did you see how worried your dad was when my mom stumbled? He cares about her. They're already friends. We just need to get them to be *more* than friends."

Ginnie let Tillie's words tumble through her mind a few times. She started to laugh and then took note of Tillie's earnest expression. "You're serious?"

"Of course." A huge smile lit Tillie's face. "Why didn't we think of this before?"

"Because we're talking about my dad. He's lame."

"He's not lame, he's quiet. He never yells, even when he's mad. Jasper yelled about everything and scared me all the time. Your dad makes me feel safe." Tillie looked her straight in the eye. "And he's nice to my mom. *Jasper was a jerk.*"

The hard edge in Tillie's voice made Ginnie wince. She could never figure out how a nice girl like Tillie had ended up with a terrible dad like Jasper Taylor.

One of Ginnie's earliest memories of Tillie was a night during their kindergarten year when Miss Amanda and Tillie showed up in the middle of the night, begging for help. Miss Amanda's mouth was bleeding and Tillie had a bruise on her cheek. Uncle Jake took one look at their faces and threatened to make Jasper Taylor pay for hurting them. When Daddy picked Tillie up to comfort her, Uncle Jake slammed the door on his way out.

She and Toran had held onto each other, trying to make sense of all the drama. Even now, six years after Mr. Taylor had left Tillie and her mom, Ginnie couldn't figure out why he had been so mean. She concentrated on Tillie's eyes, seeing something there she had never seen before. Ginnie struggled to name what she saw. Sadness? Desperation? Longing?

Tillie grabbed Ginnie's hands. "It's a great idea. You still want to be sisters, don't you?"

"Of course." Ginnie offered Tillie her most confident smile, even though she didn't feel so confident. She did still want to be sisters ... but something didn't feel quite right and she couldn't figure out what. She only knew she needed to help Tillie feel better. "Let's do it."

Tillie exhaled a breath and returned Ginnie's smile. "How are we going to get your dad to take us to the mall? My mom won't care because it's on her way home from work."

Before Ginnie could answer, the chicken coop door opened and Toran burst through. "Guess what?"

Both girls jumped. "What?"

"Princess had her babies. Five kittens. I just found them. Wanna see?"

"Sure." Ginnie scanned the henhouse and picked up the last two eggs. "Let me drop the basket off. Where are the kittens?"

"In the hay barn."

Ginnie nodded. "You two go ahead. I'll catch up."

"Cool! Can I name one?" Tillie asked, rushing out behind Toran.

Ginnie closed the bottom half of the door and left the top open. She hurried to the kitchen and set the basket in the sink. She found Uncle Ben in the dining room. "The eggs are soaking."

"Thank you." He rummaged through some boxes on the table. "Did Tillie find you?"

"Yes, and Toran just found Princess. She had her babies, so they went to see them."

Uncle Ben smiled. "I'll walk over with you. I found an old camera of Aunt Sadie's. Let's see if it still works. You three and the new kittens will make the perfect models."

"Okay." Ginnie peeked into a box of knickknacks. "Is this Aunt Sadie's stuff?"

"Most of it. Odds and ends I boxed up when we moved you and Toran into our old bedroom upstairs. I decided to clean out the boxes in my closet." He nodded toward his bedroom, which was now through the door next to the hutch. "I couldn't do it before, but it's time now."

Thinking about her mom, Ginnie sighed in sympathy. "You still miss Aunt Sadie, huh?"

"Yes. But I'll see her again." He picked up a camera case. "Until then, I'll record the important events in 'her Punkins' lives. That's what she called you and Toran." He held out his hand and drew Ginnie into a firm hug. "You two meant everything to her." He loosened his grip and smiled. "Let's go see those kittens."

She followed him through the hallway, out the front door and down the concrete stairs. "I wish I remembered Aunt Sadie, Uncle Ben. I try, really I do, but I just can't."

Uncle Ben offered her his hand. "No one expects you to. You were only two-and-a-half when Aunt Sadie passed. It's okay if your mind doesn't remember; your heart always will. Aunt Sadie was all about babies, most especially you and Toran. We would've had a dozen if we could've." He winked at Ginnie. "Though your dad and Jake were a nice bonus."

"I sometimes forget that you aren't their dad."

Uncle Ben smiled. "Love is wonderful like that. It doesn't worry about who gave birth to who, just how much time and effort is invested in another person."

Ginnie let his words sift through her mind a couple of times. "So, even though Tillie and I aren't sisters, we can love each other like sisters just because we're best friends and like spending time together?"

"Exactly like that. Sometimes the best family are really friends. Tillie's a special girl. You help each other be the best people each of you can be."

Uncle Ben's words warmed Ginnie like a cup of hot cocoa on a chilly day. "Do you think my dad will ever get married again?"

"Why are you asking?" Uncle Ben paused outside the hay barn door.

"No reason." Ginnie faced straight ahead, not knowing how to answer. "Just wondering."

7

KITTENS

Ginnie, Tillie, and Toran hammed for the camera as Uncle Ben snapped a few pictures of the kids with the kittens.

Toran loved taking pictures. He convinced Uncle Ben to let him use Aunt Sadie's camera to take a couple of pictures with Ginnie and Tillie. Toran motioned for the three of them to scoot closer together.

"Your mama was quite the shutterbug," Uncle Ben said. "You favor her like that."

Toran smiled. "Really?"

Ginnie didn't know that about her mother.

Uncle Ben nodded. "She took lots of pictures. You two were her favorite models—you and Eternal Love."

How do I favor her? Ginnie held her breath and prayed Uncle Ben would read her mind.

He came close. "You could be her twin. You look more like her all the time."

Pleasure and disappointment battled each other as bubbles whirled inside. *I want to hear something NEW. I already know I look like her.*

"I'm going to make lunch." Uncle Ben slipped the camera in his front jean pocket. "How hungry are you guys?"

"Very!" Toran and Tillie chorused together.

What about Mama? Ginnie swallowed, unable to speak. *Tell me something else.*

"What are you going to name the kittens?" Tillie asked.

"The gray one that keeps sneezing up a storm, is Storm. One of the calicos is Gingersnap. I'm not sure about the other calico and other gray one yet, but the white one's Mouse."

"Mouse?" Tillie brushed the tiny kitten. "That's an interesting name for a cat."

Toran shrugged. "He looks like a mouse."

"What do you think about naming the other calico, Cinnamon? And the gray one, Sushi? Those go along with Gingersnap and Mouse."

"Hmmm. I like that." He stroked the other calico. "She does look a bit like Cinnamon. He stroked the other gray kitten. What do you think little kitty? Do you want to be Sushi?"

Tillie giggled, gluing her eyes on Toran's face.

Ginnie stared at her twin. His dark blues eyes and short platinum blond curls made him more of a twin to Dad than to her. And his personality was quieter, like Tillie's.

Most definitely. We must've been paired on 'Opposite Day' in Heaven.

8

OPERATION SECRET SISTERS

fter lunch, Ginnie and Tillie stretched out on opposite ends of the hammock with large glasses of lemonade. The humidity was almost bearable in the shade. The small flock of five white ducks that lived on the farm played nearby in the brook.

Tillie sat upright. "So, how are we going to get your dad to take us to the mall?"

"For what?"

"How could you forget?" Tillie wagged an annoyed finger. "Remember ... so Mom and he can start dating?"

"Calm your pickles, Til." Ginnie leaned forward. "I remember now."

"Don't you *want* to be sisters?" Tillie grabbed Ginnie's wrist and shook it. "It'll be fun. We can have a slumber party every night. We can share our clothes and when you get grounded, it won't matter, because I'll be your sister and not just your friend."

Ginnie's hand flew to her hip. "Hey! I don't get in trouble that much."

"Yes, you do." Tillie frowned. "It doesn't matter to *you*; you have Toran. When I can't come over 'cause you're in trouble, I get really lonely with Mom at work." Tillie pushed Ginnie's leg playfully. "Yes you do." Tillie frownedoesn't matter to you. You have Toran. When I can't come over 'cause you're in trouble, I get really lonely with Mom at work."

Tillie pushed Ginnie's leg playfully.

"If we're sisters, it won't matter. I'll still be here."

Ginnie smirked. "You're exaggerating."

"No, I'm not." Tillie tugged the hem of Ginnie's jeans. "This idea just keeps getting better. Let's come up with a code name." Her voice almost sang with excitement.

"Now you're just being silly."

"No, I'm not." A hurt look crossed her friend's face. "You wanted a code name for talking your dad into a bigger allowance. This is even more important."

"Okay. Good point." Ginnie took a sip of lemonade.

"It'll be our new mission." A wide smile lit Tillie's lips. "Think of something."

Ginnie tapped her chin. "Like Operation: Parent Trap?"

"Naw. Sounds like a movie. Anything else?"

"How's about 'Operation: Secret Sisters?' 'OSS' for short."

"I like it. And let's be the 'Secret Sisters Club', since we already have a clubhouse." Tillie hugged her quickly, spilling their drinks a little. "Oops, sorry. Okay, we have a name. I have a plan. We just need to get your dad to the mall."

"Help me clean the hen house, I mean our *CLUBhouse*. He's a sucker for a barter. If we do a good job, he'll take us."

"Couldn't we just ask 'pretty please'?"

"*You* started this. My chores are just something else to share." Ginnie grinned. "Are you still in... Sis?"

"Of course, duh." Tillie toggled her head. "I don't mind doing chores. I just like the shade. The hen house is hot."

"Then it's settled. He'll make me do it anyway, so we ought to get a trip to the mall out of it." Ginnie slid her feet off the hammock. "It'll go twice as fast with you. And the mall has air conditioning."

"I'm in." Tillie stood and smiled, then shook her head, teasing. "The things I do for my sister."

Ginnie grinned and put a hand out.

Tillie topped it with hers.

"One, two, three. Operation: Secret Sisters. Go team!"

9

THE MALL

*D*ad and Toran made a path through the crowded mall toward the food court with Ginnie and Tillie following close on their heels. They found an open table with six chairs.

A few minutes later, Miss Amanda showed up, breathless. "Sorry, I got caught in traffic."

Tillie hugged her. "No problem, Mom."

"What are you hungry for?" Dad pulled out a chair for her. "We can't decide. Chinese, Mexican, chicken, or Italian?"

Miss Amanda set her purse on the table. "Chinese sounds good to me. I love cheese wontons."

"Why don't you two get Chinese and we'll wander around making up our minds?" Tillie suggested, wiggling her eyebrows at Ginnie. "We don't all have to have the same thing."

"Good idea, huh Daddy?" Ginnie held out her hand for money. "You guys catch up while we figure out what we want."

He gave her a twenty. "As long as you don't buy just junk."

"We won't. Thanks." She turned to Toran. "Come on."

When they got out of sight of Dad and Miss Amanda, Tillie giggled. "That wasn't so hard."

Ginnie high-fived her. "Let's get brownies and calzones."

"And king-sized cheese fries to share," Tillie added.

"What's so funny?" Toran pointed to Jose's. "I want a chimichanga."

"Nothing," Ginnie and Tillie chimed together.

When he threw them a disbelieving look and turned, Tillie and Ginnie followed him, fist bumping, and then wiggling their fingers before separating their hands. They took their time ordering in different lines, managing to eat all of their brownie and cheese fries before they got to the calzone counter.

Toran's gaze rested on the table by the fountain. "Dad's looking for us. We gotta hurry."

Ginnie frowned. *Dad should be talking to Miss Amanda, not worrying about us. Get with the plan, Daddy.* She followed Toran's stare and confirmed her brother's suspicion. She met Dad's eyes and smiled, pointing to the display case of calzones.

Dad nodded pleasantly, but she knew he expected them to hurry. Ginnie leaned toward Tillie and whispered. "He's like crazy overprotective. Are you sure you still want to be sisters?"

Tillie stared at her like she had three heads and whispered back. "Jasper hurt me and then left. At least *your* dad cares what happens to you."

Ginnie wanted to protest, but everything she thought of made her sound like a spoiled brat. How could she complain about a dad who cared too much, when Tillie's didn't care at all?

If they do get married, Daddy can worry about Tillie more than me. She grinned. *This might work out better than I thought.*

Once Dad saw them coming, he sat back in his chair and chatted easily with Miss Amanda.

Dad pulled two gift cards out of his wallet. He handed one to Toran and the other to Ginnie.

Ginnie held hers out for Tillie to see. "Cool. What for?"

Toran slipped his in his wallet. "Oma and Opa gave them to us for our birthday, remember?"

"Oh, yeah. *Sugar beets!*" Ginnie wrinkled her nose, recalling her great-grandparents making a huge deal out of their twelfth birthday the week before. Oma wanted her to pick out at least two dresses for church and Toran had been instructed to buy a new suit. Ginnie had pasted a pleasant smile on her face and thanked them even though she really wanted to groan.

"Virginia Maie." Ginnie hated it when her dad used her formal name. The quiet warning in Dad's voice didn't go unnoticed.

Ginnie resisted the urge to stomp her foot, but couldn't keep the disgust out of her voice. "I hate wearing dresses and you *know* it. Can't we shop for dresses another time? I just want to have fun today." *You're ruining all of our plans.*

His eyes narrowed. "We *were* having fun. Stop being rude."

Ginnie whirled away from him, knowing better than to blurt the truth. *Even if I wanted a new dress—which I don't—girls need to go dress shopping with their moms. And mine's not here.* She blew her bangs out of her eyes and caught Tillie miming a smile and making a twirling motion with her finger.

You don't understand either. YOU have a mom.

Hey, wait a minute...

"Daddy." Ginnie smiled the most apologetic smile she could muster and offered him her hand. He narrowed his eyes and stood, letting Ginnie pull him out of earshot of the table. He nodded to Miss Amanda as they left and waited for Ginnie to speak, an amused smile lighting his lips.

"I want to go shopping with Miss Amanda. She's fun."

A strange look crossed his face. He blinked and then nodded slowly, as if understanding her dilemma. "Sure, honey."

Sweet! Tillie will be happy I saved the day.

"Thanks." Ginnie rubbed her chin and grinned. "If there's any money left over after two dresses, can I buy something I will *want* to wear?"

"Are dresses *that* bad?" He offered her an amused smile. "You *are* a girl."

Ginnie grimaced. "I'm a tomboy."

"Saying you're a tomboy is just another way of saying you're a tough and courageous girl." He offered her a friendly wink. "Your mama was the most courageous person I've ever met. *And* she looked amazing in a dress."

Ginnie locked her eyes on his. *He never talks about Mama.* She searched for the emotion to describe his tone, but couldn't decide which nailed it best, so she followed him quietly back to their table.

Tillie offered Ginnie what was left of the calzone. Ginnie ate half and gave the rest to Dad.

He finished it as they walked to the store. Tillie elbowed Ginnie happily when Dad slowed his pace and whispered something to Miss Amanda.

Miss Amanda nodded and darted a quick look at Ginnie and Tillie. "Sure, Todd. No problem."

Dad said something Ginnie didn't hear. Miss Amanda giggled.

Wow, Daddy. Sorry I doubted you. Maybe you're not so lame after all. Ginnie exchanged grins and a "thumbs up" with Tillie. "He's asking your mom to come shopping with us because I told him it would be more fun dress shopping with your mom than just him. She can back us up when he picks out something I hate."

"Cool. We'll look like a real family." Tillie's words wrapped around her like a comfortable quilt and then made her sad. Ginnie didn't spend a lot of time thinking about what her family looked like. With her uncles, and Dad and Toran, Oma and Opa, Vi and Buzz, her family didn't look the same at any given minute, but always *felt* the same. Right ... Complete ...

Except lately. She was starting to miss Mama more and more. When they reached the Juniors section, Dad smiled at Ginnie.

Cool, he's gonna let Miss Amanda take things from here. Maybe he'll just offer to hold our bags and pretend to like what we pick out, like TV dads do.

Ginnie gave him an approving nod.

His smile grew bigger. "Toran and I'll go look at suits and leave you ladies to your shopping. Have fun." He placed a hand on her brother's shoulder, turned, and walked off with her twin before Ginnie realized her plan to feel like a family for a minute had failed miserably.

10

THE SCHEMING CONTINUES

The summer sun lit the hen house fully as Tillie opened the bottom half of the door. "Oh good! You're alone."

Ginnie laughed. "You're the only one who ever comes in to do the chickens with me, that's why this makes the perfect clubhouse."

Tillie set her basket next to Ginnie and squatted to pick up an egg. "That's true. But we need to focus on OSS. The mall wasn't a complete bust, but we need a better plan."

"I told you my dad was lame."

"That's okay. They talked when he offered everyone ice cream cones."

Ginnie added three eggs to her basket, then took a deep breath. "Well, enough of the past. What's our next plan going to be? What does *your mom* like to do?"

"My mom isn't picky. Dinner, movies, football games. *Your dad* has the problem with dating. Where did he take your mom on their first date?"

Ginnie shrugged. "I only know she was a beauty queen, she loved competing with Eternal Love, she liked taking pictures, she thought Toran and I hung the moon ... oh ... and she was stubborn." Ginnie leaned back on her heels and laughed. "And apparently, when I argue with Daddy, he thinks I'm just like her."

Tillie smiled. "You are if she was stubborn, and funny, *and* a very good friend."

"Thanks." Ginnie pushed her bangs out of her face. "And lately I keep hearing how much I look like her." She threw a disgusted glance at her chest and rolled her eyes. She liked being a tomboy and her body's betrayal irritated her.

Tillie laughed. "You waste being a girl. Your mom was a beauty queen and you don't even wear lip gloss. How did that happen?"

"Because she died." The angry whisper startled Ginnie.

She glanced at Tillie and then turned away, ashamed of the hurt that flickered across her friend's face. "I didn't mean it like that. I could care less about being a beauty queen. But I want to be a trick rider like her and Daddy won't let me." Ginnie dropped an egg roughly into the basket, cracking the one below it. *Great.*

Tillie offered her a sympathetic smile. "She sounds nice. My mom met her once, when she was still married to Jasper."

"Really?" Ginnie locked her eyes on Tillie's. "When?"

"When we were two. You know Uncle Jake and Jasper were friends in high school." Tillie grimaced while mentioning her father's name. "Uncle Ben invited us over for a barbecue when Uncle Jake was home on leave. Your dad was at work, but your mom brought you and Toran over to nap while she rode Eternal Love. Aunt Sadie kept you guys up to play with me and when your mom was done riding, they talked." Tillie sighed and picked up an egg. "They might have been friends, but Aunt Sadie died right after that and Jasper didn't want to come out to the farm anymore."

"I don't remember that."

"Me either, but Mom says Aunt Sadie was a second mom to Jasper. After Aunt Sadie died, Jasper started drinking. That's when things got bad." Tillie took a sudden interest in some hens squawking and sat back on the heels of her sneakers.

Ginnie tried to swallow the lump forming in her throat.

"When Jasper hurt us, your family were the only ones she trusted to help us."

"I'm glad she thought to come to the farm that night. That's when we became like sisters. I was sorry when Uncle Ben helped your mom find the apartment and you guys moved out."

"Me too. But if we can get our folks to fall in love, Mom and I can move back in." Tillie put an egg in the basket and smiled at Ginnie. "My mom's a nice person and so's your dad. They need to be together and not just so we can be sisters. They could both use a good friend."

"Yeah. Dad doesn't act like he misses Mama, but I know he does." Ginnie glanced at Tillie and then the door. "I think the reason he ditched us was because he felt sorry for me that I don't have a mom. I don't really need one, because I have Vi, but I like your mom and with her around, he won't worry about me so much. I hate how overprotective he is."

Tillie chewed her lip. "I like that about him."

"You won't when he hovers over *you* all the time. He even told me I can't date until I'm thirty-seven. Not that I want to, boys are gross." Ginnie rolled her eyes. "But seriously, what is our new plan going to be?"

Tillie opened her mouth and jumped to her feet, squealing. "I've got it! A picnic! Lunch, talking, and maybe even kissing."

"Daddy treats your mom like Vi, who's like his little sister. He's *not* going to kiss his sister." Ginnie leaned forward. "Vi calls him and Uncle Jake 'Neanderthals' for a reason. They enjoy picking on Vi's boyfriends. And remember when your mom dated that Albert guy? Even Daddy teased him."

Tillie sucked in a horrified breath. "If they start dating, do you think Uncle Jake will be nice, or not?"

"I dunno." Ginnie gathered more eggs. "But Uncle Ben will make him behave if they *do* get serious."

Tillie groaned. "Uncle Jake better not mess up our plans."

"We haven't made any plans, but a picnic is out."

"Why?"

"How's a picnic gonna happen?" Ginnie waved her hand. "Hand

them a lunch basket and tell them to go away and not come back until they want to get married?"

"What about dinner at a restaurant?" Tillie suggested.

Ginnie shrugged. "Or a movie?"

"No, we want them to talk." Tillie scrunched her eyebrows in thought.

"We need to get them to take *us* somewhere." Ginnie suggested. "They aren't going to go off by themselves."

"Fine, where do *we* want to go?" Tillie asked.

Ginnie didn't hesitate. "Go-carting."

"Good idea. And fun, too. So *when* are we going?" Tillie squatted next to Ginnie and brushed straw off an egg.

Ginnie shrugged again. "Let's ask Daddy."

They gathered the rest of the eggs and rushed into the farmhouse to drop their baskets off in the kitchen. They nearly ran into Buzz, Uncle Ben's son.

"Have you seen my dad?" Ginnie asked.

"He's loading Dad's truck with hay."

Ginnie motioned Tillie to follow. "Thanks, Buzz."

"No prob."

They hurried through the dining room and out the front door.

Ginnie and Tillie rushed down the gray-painted concrete steps and sprinted between Dad's green sedan and Vi's purple convertible VW bug.

Uncle Ben's loaded truck was headed down the lane, followed by a cloud of dust.

Disappointment clouded Tillie's face. "Now what?"

Ginnie just shrugged.

11

E-E-E-E-E!

*G*innie stared at the dust moving down the lane. "Nuts! No telling when he'll be back."

"Look! There he is!" Tillie pointed at the hay barn and grabbed Ginnie's hand. They raced toward Dad and Uncle Jake, who were loading light green alfalfa hay bales into the back of Uncle Jake's black truck.

"We thought you were in the truck," Ginnie said, her voice more accusing than friendly.

"Is something wrong?" Dad arched an eyebrow. "You know I never leave without telling you good-bye."

Ginnie sifted through her memories. She couldn't recall one time her dad had left without saying, "Goodbye, I love you." Even when he was rushed or aggravated with her. "Nothing's wrong. We just wanted to know if you'd take us to ride go-carts?"

"Right now?" Dad's brows knitted together.

"No, just soon."

"Soon, as in *today*? I have to be at work at two. And I have work here before I leave."

They hadn't thought that far ahead. Ginnie tossed a frustrated look at Tillie.

"Saturday would be the earliest." Dad wiped his forehead with his leather glove. "We work nights today and tomorrow."

Tillie smiled. "Saturday would be perfect."

Dad returned her smile. "I have a couple things to do on Saturday. I'll have to get back to you on when and possibly 'if'—I may not be able to."

Uncle Jake tugged Ginnie's braid. "If you're going go-carting, I'm in. I'll take you."

"No," Ginnie and Tillie said a little too sharply, together.

Uncle Jake pulled his hand back as if Ginnie had bit him.

Dad tilted his head, waiting for an explanation.

Ginnie glanced at Tillie, eyes wide.

"No?" Uncle Jake echoed, frowning.

Ginnie's cheeks warmed. "I mean. Sure, Uncle Jake. We like go-karting with you, we just wanted *Daddy* to drive us." Ginnie slipped her arms around Dad's waist and met his curious look with the most innocent one she could muster. "I've just missed him lately. I wanted to spend time with him. But you can come too."

Dad hugged her back, squeezing the side of her face against his ribs. "I just took you to the mall last night, but how can I say 'no' to that?"

Uncle Jake rolled his eyes at her. "Yah, how?"

Ginnie wasn't sure if she heard teasing or sarcasm, but when Dad winked at her, she knew she'd won *him* over at least.

Tillie giggled. Uncle Jake squeezed Tillie's shoulder. "Fine, I won't be insulted. But if you're going with your dad, Tillie's going to be my date, okay Turtle?"

Tillie's eyes shined. "Sure. And Toran can be my mom's—we could invite her too, right?"

Uncle Jake shrugged. "That works for me."

Ginnie looked at her dad. "Okay?"

"Why wouldn't it be?" He changed the subject a little too fast, and shrugged. "Are you done with your chores?"

"Yes, sir." Ginnie took a step back. "Eggs are in the sink."

"Can you two wash and sort them? We need to finish stacking bales. Send Toran over if you see him."

"Yes, sir," Ginnie and Tillie chorused.

Dad laughed. "In stereo even. Maybe Ginnie needs a triplet. What do you think, Gin?" Tillie's grin grew so huge Ginnie thought her face might crack in two.

"Tillie would make a perfect sister. And we wear the same size clothes."

"Very practical thinking. Two girls, one wardrobe." Dad lifted a bale. "Start the eggs please."

Tillie's eyes widened in delight. She and Ginnie fist-bumped when they left the barn. "E-e-e-e-!" Tillie squealed as Ginnie high-fived her. "Awesome sauce!"

They grabbed each other's hands and happy-danced together.

12

OSS IS ON!

Tillie slipped into the hen house the next morning just as Ginnie finished gathering the eggs.

"You're late today. I'm done in here."

"Sorry, Mom's car wouldn't start. We had to get a jump." Tillie rushed through the explanation so fast Ginnie had to let the words go through her mind again to understand what her friend had said. "Mom said she'd come go-karting with us tomorrow, so how are we gonna further our mission for OSS?"

Ginnie shrugged. "I dunno, I hadn't thought about that."

Tillie put her hands on her hips. "Why not?"

"Calm your pickles, Tillie. You were there yesterday when Daddy asked me if you should be my triplet." Ginnie rolled her eyes and smiled. "That means OSS'll work."

Tillie slid her hands down her jeans. "Sorry, it's all I've been thinking about."

"No prob. Here." Ginnie handed her one of the two wire egg baskets and opened the bottom half of the door. "What are you so worried about? You practically live here anyway."

Tillie followed Ginnie out of the hen house and stopped. "Do you think when your dad marries my mom, he'll adopt me? So I can be Tillie West and not Tillie Taylor anymore?"

Ginnie shrugged. "I guess so. If you want him to."

"I *do* want him to." Tillie locked her eyes on Ginnie's. "More than anything." The urgency in her voice sent goose pimples across Ginnie's arms. She turned from Tillie, rubbed the bumps away and started toward the farmhouse.

By the time they joined everybody at the breakfast table, Ginnie had repeated "I *do* want him to" several times in her mind, trying to figure out the tone Tillie used when she said 'do'. It hovered between longing and desperation.

Tillie sat next to Ginnie, twirling her long hair around her finger, over and over. When Dad showed up with Uncle Jake and Toran, Tillie dropped her hand into her lap and smiled.

Uncle Jake snatched a piece of bacon. "Smells delicious."

"Thank you. But join us for a blessing before you eat that bacon." Uncle Ben arched an eyebrow, his tone friendly. "I raised you better than that."

"Yes, sir." Uncle Jake rolled his eyes and dropped the bacon on his plate. "It's your own fault—if you weren't such a good cook, we wouldn't sneak bites."

Uncle Ben chuckled. "No need to sneak. There's plenty for everybody."

Tillie giggled. "I like that about you guys, you're nice to everybody, family or not."

Dad winked at her. "Who's not family? You work just as hard with Ginnie that I've been thinking I should probably give *you* an allowance as well."

Tillie's cheeks pinked. "I like helping her."

"Even so, I'm giving you a bonus for helping her with the chicken coop. That's hot work and we'll be out go-karting tomorrow ..." Dad pulled out his chair and sat. "We can do a little shopping as well."

Something about the way Tillie's eyes shined brought new understanding to the urgency Ginnie heard in her voice earlier. She turned to Tillie and fist-bumped with her under the table.

OSS is s-o-o-o on!

13

MOM'S JOURNAL

illie scooted her chair back and looked up from her drive-thru burger and fries on their dining room table when Mom's phone rang.

Mom glanced at the number and jumped up. "Be right back." She walked quickly to her room and shut the door.

What's that about? Tillie finished her fries and jiggled her foot, waiting for Mom to return.

Mom came back as Tillie stood to clear the table, crumpling a wrapper. "Who was that?"

"Just someone from work. I need to go out for a bit. Can you clean the kitchen and fold the clothes from the dryer?" Mom didn't wait for an answer. She kissed Tillie's forehead, grabbed her purse and left.

After snapping on the TV, Tillie dumped out the basket onto the couch. She did laundry all the time with Ginnie at the farm and didn't mind. Doing it alone wasn't any fun. *Where did Mom go?* It wasn't like her mom to rush off for private phone calls or mysterious errands.

Get a grip, Til. She'll be back.

Tillie folded clothes and watched a show about teens running a cooking show. During the commercial, she put away her socks and then Mom's. As she pushed her mother's socks in a drawer, Tillie's fingernails brushed a blue, leather-bound book. Silver lettering caught her eye. "Journal"

Knowing she shouldn't, Tillie pulled it out, glanced around the room and sat on the edge of Mom's bed. She opened the book and skimmed the first page:

DEC 28

Dear Journal,

I'm going to try once again to keep a journal since Vi went to the trouble of buying me such a nice one for Christmas. Maybe something exciting will happen that I can record. If not, I'll fill you in with what Tillie does—she's my eleven year-old daughter and the reason I can get up most mornings. She's the only good thing I got from my marriage with Jasper Taylor. ☹

Tillie smiled at the frowning face next to Jasper's name.

She skimmed a few entries and then remembered her mom crying the other night as she slammed this book shut. Tillie flipped to the last couple entries, hoping to find out why Mom was crying.

Dear Journal,

I don't know what to do. My life's a mess. All I ever wanted for as long as I can remember was to feel safe in my own home, with my family. My alcoholic father and spineless mother made that impossible.

When Jasper convinced me that because we came from the same kind of backgrounds, we could do better, I wanted to believe him. That didn't last long and now our daughter has the same legacy—well, better because I kicked Jasper to the curb. But I can see the same loss in her that I feel in me.

At least Tillie gets to spend time with the West family—a decent family. It's nice to know she's safe and cared for when I'm not with her. I just want her to feel safe all the time.

Today I got horrible news...

A scribbled line ran down the page a couple of inches.

That must be when she closed the book. Tillie scanned the next entry.

Today was better. I met Todd and the kids at the mall. He asked me to help Ginnie find some dresses. He got the feeling she felt weird shopping with her dad and asked if I would mind offering a feminine touch. Of course I didn't mind at all. Poor kid, she has the opposite problem from Tillie.

It was fun to have 2 daughters to shop with. Only she REALLY doesn't like dresses. I wonder what her mom, the beauty queen, would think about that? 😄

She only agreed to the two dresses we bought because I fussed over them. They really did look nice on her, but she didn't seem too happy, until Todd let her buy a t-shirt with a horse on it. Then she perked up. She's a cowgirl at heart, I guess.

Tillie asked me for a horse. If I could afford to care for one, I'd get her one in a heartbeat. I would love to ride with her. All girls should have horses, and a dad that's good to them and makes them feel safe.

Tillie smiled. *When you marry DT, I'll get both.*

A car door slammed.

Tillie flinched.

Mom! She shoved the book back in the drawer and pushed the socks on top of it. She rushed through the living room and peeked out the window. Mom's parking space was empty.

Puzzled, she glanced around. A car honked. *The TV! Whew.*

Tillie took another look at the empty parking spot and rushed back to the journal, giggling nervously at her overactive imagination.

Maybe she'll say why she was crying in the next entry. She fished the book out and flicked it open to the last entry.

Tillie wants me to ride go-carts with Jake, Todd, and his kids on Saturday. Jake is such a character. Sometimes I wished I'd met him before Jasper. I actually met them at the same dance, but since I went to the dance with Jasper, I couldn't very well flirt with Jake. If I'd known Jasper would turn into an abusive alcoholic like his father and mine, I'd have begged Jake to take me home that night and refused to ever see Jasper again. Jake would make such a great dad.

NO! NO! NO! Tillie slammed the book shut when she realized that was the end of the passage. Tears burned her eyes. *Mom, you need to fall in love with DT, NOT Uncle Jake!*

14

RIDING GO-CARTS

$\mathcal{A}$re you sure they're coming?" Ginnie asked Dad for the second time, searching the go-cart parking lot.

He shrugged and leaned against the painted blue brick building. "That's what Amanda told Uncle Ben." Dad gave a friendly wink. "Quit worrying, they're not even late, we're five minutes early."

Ginnie put her hands on her hips and looked him straight in the eye. "You know, Daddy, if I had a cell phone, I could call Amanda and Tillie and make sure they're all right."

He chuckled. "Nice try. And that's *Miss* Amanda to you. She's an adult. Be respectful."

"Vi's an adult and I call her Vi."

"Vi's my cousin and that makes her *your* cousin. Cousins don't have a title in their name."

"Okay, but a cellphone is still a good idea."

"Not today."

Toran shook his head. "Dad, you really need to join this century. We're practically the only kids at school without phones."

"Talk to me when you're the *only* ones without a phone." Dad smiled and tousled Toran's hair. "Though it probably won't do you much good."

Uncle Jake threw back his head and laughed. "Sorry guys. I tried to talk him into cell phones for your birthday, but your old man is a stick-in-the-mud."

"And since I'm your younger brother, I guess that makes you Peter Pan." Dad held the door open for Ginnie and motioned for her to go in. "I'll get my kids cell phones when you get *your* kids cell phones."

Uncle Jake frowned. "Very funny."

"Really?" Ginnie squealed. "Daddy, please let him get us cell phones. Pretty please?"

"Yah, Uncle Jake, that's really cool." Toran high-fived their uncle and turned to Dad.

"You're too young for cell phones." Dad narrowed his eyes at Uncle Jake and turned on his 'lecture' voice. "Thanks a lot, Bro. I really appreciate the back-up here."

Ginnie glanced at Toran. She didn't miss the slight shake of his head indicating she should stay out of their bickering. She clamped her mouth shut.

"Just because I don't happen to agree with you, doesn't make *me* wrong." Uncle Jake followed Toran through the door. "Toran's right, you need to get with *this* century."

"You didn't even buy yourself one. Quit trying to make me look bad."

Uncle Jake rolled his eyes. "I'm waiting for you to change your mind. Four phones cost just a tad more than one." Uncle Jake buffed his fingernails against his purple polo. "Coz I'm a cool uncle like that."

"Stop rolling your eyes at me. You know I hate it when Ginnie does. She gets it from you." Dad stuck a thumb in his jean's pocket. "And bribing my kids makes you cool ... *not*."

Ginnie grinned. "*Letting* him bribe us makes *you* the best dad in the world!"

Uncle Jake snorted and fist-bumped with her.

Dad wagged a scolding finger. He pointed it at his royal blue T-shirt that read 'World's Best Dad', a present from Ginnie for last

Father's Day. "What happened to me being: 'the best dad in the whole world' because I let you have Calliope?"

"Well, that's true, of course." Ginnie leaned against him and hugged him hard, tossing him her most sincere smile. "But cell phones would *keep* you as the best dad ... ever."

Dad laughed. "You're too much like your uncle. And since I'm the *only* dad you have, I'll take my chances. No cell phones."

"At least we tried." Toran mumbled. "Say Dad, the MP3 players you got us were cool and all, but I really need my own computer. The one in the study is a dinosaur and I'm not allowed to use it anyway. I have just about enough allowance saved. Can we look at computers today? Please?"

"Can we just stay focused on riding go-karts for now?" Dad scanned the lobby. "Do you want your own go-kart or do you want to share?"

"My own!" Toran said.

"Share!" Ginnie replied. "With Tillie. We'll take turns driving."

Dad smiled. "Okay. Jake?"

"My own. And I'm challenging you to a race. Winner gets their way with the cell phones."

"No way, but if you want 'good uncle points', I'll let you pay for the rentals." Dad turned to Ginnie and winked. "I drove. He pays. It's all good."

"So you think my wallet's bottomless? I don't have kids so I can afford to spoil yours." He winked at Ginnie. "At least *they* appreciate me."

"I *really* appreciate you. I'll even let you donate to the 'Toran needs a new computer' fund." Toran turned to Dad and elbowed him gently in the ribs. "And you can donate as well. You wouldn't want Uncle Jake to look like the more generous contributor, now would you?"

"Since I pay your allowance ..." Dad elbowed him back. "He'd have to be awfully generous to outdo me."

Uncle Jake smirked and pulled out his wallet. "Fine, I'll rent the carts and you help Toran with the computer. We both get cool points. Win, win."

Dad shrugged. "If you really want to be nice, pay for Amanda and Tillie as well. I had planned to offer. Amanda had to take her car to the mechanic earlier this week."

Cool. Dad's paying for Miss Amanda and Tillie like a real date. Ginnie smiled at him. *Well, he would've if he didn't trick Uncle Jake into it. Daddy's going right along with our plans.*

"Sure, no problemo." Uncle Jake and Toran walked over to the rental counter.

Turning toward the door, Ginnie caught sight of Miss Amanda and Tillie. "Daddy, they're here!" Ginnie ran over to them. "Hey, Miss Amanda." She grabbed Tillie's hand and pulled her halfway across the room. "Daddy offered to pay for your guys' tickets and everything. Just like a real date."

Tillie seemed confused, but grinned when Dad waved at her. "Oh, good."

Toran joined Dad and Miss Amanda. "Wanna race?"

Miss Amanda nodded. "Sure, Toran, you're on."

Uncle Jake came over and offered a ride bracelet to Miss Amanda. She smiled brightly and took it. "Thanks, Jake. You didn't have too."

"You're welcome." Uncle Jake leaned in toward Miss Amanda's ear and whispered something.

She pushed his chest and laughed.

Tillie spun away, but not before Ginnie saw her lip tremble.

15

TORAN'S CLOSE CALL

*W*hat's the matter?" Ginnie whispered. "You look like you're going to cry."

Tillie blinked again. She glared at Uncle Jake and turned her back on the adults.

"Tillie? What's wrong?" Ginnie walked around to face her friend.

"Uncle Jake's ruining *everything*."

Ginnie glanced at her uncle, who was still joking with Dad and Miss Amanda. "How?"

"My mom's in love with him." She spoke so forcefully, spit flew from her mouth.

"No way!"

"*Yes* way. Now we won't ever get to be sisters." She wiped her eyes and kept glaring.

Uncle Jake winked at Miss Amanda and then elbowed Dad when Toran laughed at him.

Ginnie felt a pang of disappointment and then smiled. "Hey, if that's true, it's not all bad. Uncle Jake seems to like your mom. We could be cousins, which is just as good."

Tillie shook her head. "No, it's not."

"Yes, it is. That's what Uncle Ben says about his four kids. Vi and

Buzz are Daddy and Uncle Jake's cousins. They're all friends. Quit worrying. It's all good."

"Girls, let's go. Our carts are ready," Dad called.

Tillie cast an appraising glance at the group across the way. "You promise being cousins will be just as good?"

Ginnie nodded. "Of course. We'll still be best friends whether we're cousins or sisters."

Tillie's eyes lit as they walked to Uncle Jake, who held up their ride bracelets.

Uncle Jake handed Dad Ginnie's bracelet and offered to help Tillie put hers on.

Tillie held out her wrist. Uncle Jake picked the tab off the tape and stuck the neon orange bracelet around her friend's wrist.

Ginnie held her own wrist out to Dad and watched Tillie eyeing Uncle Jake. She giggled. *Tillie just needs a magnifying glass and Uncle Jake won't have ANY secrets.*

Ginnie followed Tillie to the first green double go-cart. Tillie called the driver's side.

Dad told them to buckle before he slid into a blue cart behind Toran's red one. Uncle Jake hopped into a black one after Miss Amanda chose a yellow.

Toran challenged Ginnie and Tillie to a race after he started his motor. They drove their carts to a smaller oval race track and waited for the signal light to flash green.

Tillie fumbled with the pedal as Toran drove ahead. He stayed in the lead all the way around the track.

After he beat them, Ginnie offered to race again. "But let's do it on the bigger track."

"You're on," Toran said.

Tillie pulled over to the 'pit stop area' and switched places with Ginnie. Ginnie drove their cart to the main track and lined it up with Toran's.

"On your mark, get set, GO!" all three squealed.

Toran pulled ahead and Ginnie stomped the pedal all the way to the floor. She pulled ahead of him on the next turn. He caught up when they turned the other way. Neck-and-neck they stayed most of the way, dodging tires lining the track as they weaved in and out of the multitude of curves. Ginnie passed Toran as he rounded the curve going into the finish line.

She glanced at her brother. He jerked the wheel and sent his cart flying up the side of a tire. She hit the brake and watched, open-mouthed, as his cart continued forward—bouncing him against the restraints of his seat belt. His cart stopped, the back wheel of the cart stuck in the middle of one of the tires. He rocked against his seat belt to loosen the cart. It didn't budge.

Just as Ginnie unfastened her belt, Dad bolted by on foot, barking, "Stay. Buckle up!" Ginnie hooked the belt back together.

Miss Amanda stopped her cart next to Ginnie and Tillie. "Are you okay?"

Ginnie nodded.

Tillie exhaled. "We're fine, Mom."

Uncle Jake ran past.

Dad helped Toran out of the cart. The three of them lifted the cart and set it back on the track. Dad pointed between Ginnie, Tillie, and Toran. "Are you guys okay?"

"Yes, sir." All three answered.

He nodded. "No more racing. Just drive the carts."

"But ..." Ginnie protested, then stopped when Dad snapped his head toward her in warning.

She swallowed hard. "Yes, sir."

"He's fine, Todd. Chill out." Uncle Jake pushed Dad gently past the carts.

Dad's eyes darted between the three kids. "No more racing."

Ginnie waited for Dad to turn away before she rolled her eyes.

Toran started his cart.

Miss Amanda smiled and held a hand out to Toran. "Be more careful, okay?"

Toran squeezed her hand and grinned. "Got it."

Miss Amanda motioned for him to pull in front of her. She turned to the girls. "Go ahead of me."

Ginnie and Tillie exchanged smiles and giggles. Ginnie turned the wheel and followed Toran over the finish line. "You know, if Uncle Jake gets to be your dad, you'll get to have a lot more fun than we do. He doesn't get as crazy as Daddy."

Tillie didn't smile like Ginnie hoped she would. Instead, Tillie shrugged, and said nothing.

16

OSC

*G*innie and Tillie spent the rest of their session speeding around the tracks, alternating between driving and passengering.

Dad finally relented and let them race around the oval track, but insisted they be careful.

"Got it," Ginnie reassured him for the fifth time, rolling her eyes when he drove past.

"You know that bugs him," Tillie warned.

Ginnie shrugged. "It bugs *me* that he's so smothering. You're lucky. Sometimes I wish Uncle Jake was my dad. He doesn't worry like Daddy and *he* knows how to have fun."

"Stop saying that. Your dad *is* fun." Tillie pursed her lips and turned away.

"Says *you*. You're a worrywart too." Ginnie rolled her eyes again and smiled when Uncle Jake drove up beside them. "Wanna race, Uncle Jake? The warden says it's okay."

He laughed. "Sure, but that's my name for him. *You* get to call him 'Daddy'."

"Whatever." Ginnie threw him an exaggerated eye roll.

They lined up.

"Hey! I want to race, too." Miss Amanda pulled up beside Uncle Jake.

He grinned. "Cool. A three-way race. Being the gentleman I am, I will apologize in advance for leaving you ladies in the dust, before we even start."

"Oh, brother." Miss Amanda winked at the girls, and then shook her head at Uncle Jake. "I think your ego needs its own cart, Jacob West."

"Is that so, Miss Amanda Taylor?"

She stared him down. "That's so."

"Ouch!" Uncle Jake waited for the two carts to line up on either side of him. "Then I take back my aforementioned apology. Eat ... my ... dust."

When the signal light turned green, Ginnie stomped on the gas pedal and pulled ahead. Miss Amanda led Uncle Jake by a tire. Ginnie grinned and waved as she drove faster.

Uncle Jake winked at her, slowed down long enough to get out of the middle, zipped diagonally to the right of both carts, and hit the accelerator. He weaved back towards them and past Ginnie. Miss Amanda clenched her jaw and leaned forward.

Ginnie slowed the go-cart.

"What are you doing?" Tillie yelled. "Go faster."

"I want your mom to win." Ginnie pointed to Miss Amanda, who was gaining on Uncle Jake.

They followed as the two carts in front of them took turns leading and falling behind. Finally, Miss Amanda crossed the finish line first.

Ginnie stopped next to Uncle Jake and grinned. "What was that about eating your dust?"

Uncle Jake laughed. "I decided to let her win. It was the right thing to do."

"Yeah, right. She beat you fair and square." Ginnie jerked a thumb at Tillie. "We're witnesses."

The chime to end their session sounded.

Uncle Jake shrugged. "I'd offer a rematch, Amanda, but we gotta go." He turned to Ginnie. "Put your cart up. We'll meet you inside."

Ginnie drove around him and stopped the cart when she couldn't go any further.

Tillie motioned for Ginnie to follow her. "Come on."

Ginnie followed her to the restroom. "You know Tillie, if your mom marries Uncle Jake, we'll probably get cell phones."

Tillie scrunched her nose. "Why would you say that?"

"Uncle Jake was going to get Toran and me phones for our birthday, but Daddy said no. He told Uncle Jake he'd buy us cell phones as soon as Uncle Jake bought his kids cell phones."

"But Uncle Jake doesn't have any kids," Tillie protested.

"Keep up." Ginnie shook her head and smiled. "*You'll* be his kid. Uncle Jake'll buy *you* a phone and then Daddy has to buy *us* phones. How cool is that?" She grabbed Tillie's hands and happy-danced. "We get to be cousins *and* we get cell phones. This is getting better all the time."

Ginnie waited for her words to sink into Tillie's understanding.

A faint smile lit Tillie's lips and grew bigger. "And I can still move to the farm?"

"Of course. Nothing will change except Uncle Jake will be your dad—and he's cooler. That might be even better."

Tillie nodded slowly, her smile becoming brighter as the idea took root. "I guess we can change OSS to OSC, 'Operation: Secret Cousins,' right?"

Ginnie hugged her. "You can still move into my room *and* we get cellphones. Win, win."

Tillie hugged her back. "Okay. Uncle Jake's always nice to me. And he let my mom win, so that means he's gotta like her too, right?"

"Right."

"Cool."

The door opened and they waited for a woman with a little boy to pass. Ginnie followed Tillie into the lobby. *I might have lost a sister, but I've gained a cousin. It's all good.*

Ginnie stopped short, bumping Tillie as her friend froze like a statue in front of her. Tillie didn't move.

In the lobby, Uncle Jake slipped his arms around the waist of a pretty woman with light brown curls that she'd never seen before. The woman reached her arms around his neck and kissed Uncle Jake's cheek. Ginnie's heart dropped to her toes.

17

NOW WHAT?

*G*innie stumbled as she took a step. She grabbed for Tillie to steady herself. Tillie's fists clenched. Her biceps hardened as Ginnie straightened. "Sorry, Til."

Tillie stayed frozen. Unmoving. Like someone had cast a spell of immobility on her. The only sign of movement was a pointless blink to forbid the river of tears gathering behind her lids. Ginnie knew if she didn't think of something to distract Tillie, and think it up quick, Tillie would dissolve into a weeping puddle of girl.

As sick as Ginnie felt watching the unknown woman kiss her uncle, the ghostly pallor to Tillie's skin warned of an even worse storm brewing in Tillie's mind.

Uncle Jake leaned down and returned the woman's kiss.

She pulled him closer.

He smiled bigger and kissed her again.

Ginnie's heart pounded in her ears. She crossed her arms in front of her chest and marched past Tillie, intent on making the kissing stop.

Miss Amanda beat Ginnie across the room, flashing a welcoming smile to the woman torpedoing all of their efforts.

Uncle Jake took a step back and slipped his arm around the

woman's waist, pulling her next to him, hip to hip. The top of her head reached just past his shoulder.

She was even prettier up close. Uncle Jake grinned at the woman and then nodded to Miss Amanda. "Clarissa, this is my good friend Amanda, and my niece, Ginnie."

After Ginnie felt her cheeks heat, she placed 'Clarissa' as the friendly voice she'd heard on the phone that called occasionally when Uncle Jake was at work or doing chores on the farm. She'd given several messages to Uncle Jake from Miss Clarissa and teased him often about wanting to meet his mysterious girlfriend.

But not like this!

Ginnie gave herself a mental slap upside the head.

Of course. Uncle Jake's been dating Miss Clarissa for almost a month. He's being nice to Miss Amanda because they're friends, nothing more.

She turned to Tillie, who stood just as Ginnie had left her.

Maybe someone DID cast a spell of immobility on her.

Miss Amanda shook Miss Clarissa's hand as Uncle Jake continued the introductions: Dad, Toran, Tillie.

Tillie.

Ginnie eyed her friend, crossing the room quickly to whisper in Tillie's ear. "It's okay. We'll figure it out." She snatched at Tillie's clenched fist and dragged her back into the restroom, ignoring Dad's invitation to talk with Miss Clarissa.

She had to get Tillie out of there ... and the sooner the better.

18

IT CAN STILL WORK OUT

Glancing between the restroom door and Tillie, Ginnie was thankful she thought of the one place Dad wouldn't follow them. She didn't want to explain Tillie's freaked out expression or OSS. Hugging her friend, Ginnie whispered. "It's okay."

"No it's not." Tillie wiped her tears. "We're never gonna be sisters *or* cousins."

Ginnie leaned against one of the ceramic sinks trying to think of a way to make Uncle Jake kissing Miss Clarissa all right. *Fine time to introduce us to your mystery girlfriend, Uncle Jake. You couldn't pick a better place to sneak a smooch, like, oh, say, in the cafeteria at school?*

Fury bubbled.

Just when we're trying to get Daddy and Miss Amanda together. Hey, wait a minute ... Miss Amanda.

Ginnie peeked in the mirror and forced her snarling frown into a passable smile. "Your mom didn't seem upset at meeting Miss Clarissa. Why did you say she was in love with Uncle Jake?"

"Because she wrote in her journal that she wished she'd met Uncle Jake instead of Jasper, and that he'd make a good dad. But he likes *Clarissa*." Tillie spat Miss Clarissa's name like she would a mouthful of brussel sprouts.

Ginnie took a step back, bumping into the sink. "You read her journal?"

"She was crying and lied about *why* she was crying." Tillie planted her hands on her hips, her look daring Ginnie to argue. "I have a right to know why my very own mom was crying."

Ginnie grabbed Tillie's hand and grinned. "Don't you get it? This was just a big mistake. Uncle Jake and your mom, they're just friends."

"But she wrote ..." Tillie stopped short. Her eyes brightened. "Wait a minute." Understanding lit her eyes. She snapped her fingers. "If Mom's okay with Uncle Jake dating Clarissa, then OSS might still work out."

The restroom door opened slowly.

Ginnie shoved Tillie into a stall, whispering. "Wipe your face and try to look happy."

Tillie lifted the hem of her pink T-shirt to dry her eyes and closed the purple stall door.

Miss Amanda stepped toward Ginnie. "Where's Tillie? Are you guys okay?"

Ginnie pointed at the stall. "Sure, why wouldn't we be?"

"Because you left in a hurry. Jake wants you to meet Clarissa. He's leaving with her in a minute and your dad asked me to check on you."

"We're fine—just had to make a quick stop before we go shopping. You're coming, aren't you?" Ginnie tossed her a big grin and hurried to explain when Miss Amanda shook her head. "Daddy said he's treating Tillie to a shopping trip because she helped me clean the hen house."

"He didn't say anything about that." Miss Amanda glanced at the mirror and brushed her fingers through her hair. "Tils, you okay?"

"Yeah."

Ginnie smiled at Miss Amanda's reflection in the mirror.

She has pretty green eyes. Why haven't I noticed that before?

"Daddy's forgetful like that. But it's okay. If Uncle Jake is leaving with Miss Clarissa, then there's room in our car for you and Tillie."

Ginnie grabbed Miss Amanda's hand and dragged her out the door. "So, is Miss Clarissa nice?"

"Yes, and Jake seems happy, so I'm happy for him. He deserves a nice girlfriend."

"Why didn't *you* ever date him?" The words slipped out before Ginnie could stop them.

Miss Amanda looked away. "Jake and I?" She shook her head. "We have too much history to date. We're just friends." They stopped talking when they reached Uncle Jake and Miss Clarissa.

Miss Clarissa clasped both hands over Ginnie's and pumped her hand, smiling wide. "I am so happy to finally meet you. You're every bit as sweet as you sound on the phone." She glanced at Uncle Jake. "Your uncle brags on you all the time."

"We should talk ... without *him*." Ginnie winked at Uncle Jake when he rolled his eyes.

He put his arm around Miss Clarissa's waist and swept her toward the door. "I think Clarissa's met enough of my friends and family for one day." He touched the brim of his green baseball cap, gave a quick nod, and kept going out the front door.

"Ja-a-a-ke." Miss Clarissa's protest fell on deaf ears. "It was nice meeting all of you," she called over her shoulder.

Uncle Jake lifted his hand and waved. "See ya."

Miss Amanda turned to Dad. "What's his hurry?"

Dad chuckled. "He doesn't want to give me any more time than necessary for payback. He treated me pretty badly when I dated. He doesn't believe that turnabout's fair play."

Ginnie scrunched her nose. "What does that mean?"

Toran laughed. "It means Uncle Jake can dish it out, but he can't take it."

"Oh." Ginnie looked Dad in the eye. "Did you date a lot?"

Dad shrugged. "Not a lot, and once I met your mama; I didn't see any other woman."

She wanted to ask him if he saw Miss Amanda, but changed the subject instead. "Say, Daddy. I thought since Uncle Jake left with Miss Clarissa, Miss Amanda should ride with us to the shopping center.

You told Tillie you were giving her a bonus for helping me and Toran could look at computers. Miss Amanda could come with us, *right?*"

When he looked from her to Miss Amanda, Ginnie threw her arms around his waist. "You're the best dad in the whole world, even if you won't let us have cell phones."

She peeked out from under his arm just in time to see Miss Amanda put her hand over her mouth to stifle a laugh.

Dad's chest heaved as he chuckled. "Virginia Maie Stratton West, *the second*, you don't play fair. How am I supposed to say 'no' to that?"

"You're not." Ginnie giggled and sent a quick "thumbs up" to a grinning Tillie, who walked up behind her mom just then.

19

COMPUTER SHOPPING

*G*innie and Tillie stood in the computer store, watching Toran's fingers fly over the keyboard of a blue laptop. Dad approached him. "Did you find what you are looking for?"

"Maybe. But it costs more than I have. Maybe a different store would have this on sale?"

"Possibly." Dad placed a hand on Toran's shoulder. "Or you may have to wait another month or two and save your money. How much are you needing?"

"That depends on the features. I really want the extra memory and speed of that red one, but this black one has amazing graphics." Toran typed a new command. "Check this out."

Ginnie took a step closer as brilliant 3-D color burst from the monitor in the form of dozens of exotic birds flying around a bird sanctuary.

"Wow, Toran. That's amazing!" Miss Amanda leaned over Toran's other shoulder. "Todd, look at the definition and colors. It's almost as good as being there."

Toran's smile grew.

The parrots and other birds cawed. They heard swooshing as the birds flew by.

"It would be the ultimate gaming experience. Can you imagine playing King's World or Jewel Quest on this?" Toran practically gushed.

"Or even watching a cooking demo or a music video." Miss Amanda seemed as excited as Toran. "What kind of graphics card does it have?"

Toran launched into the virtues of that graphics card versus the one on the red computer.

Ginnie glanced at Tillie. *Boring.* She stifled a giggle when Dad suddenly became more interested in the computers after Miss Amanda tested another laptop.

Tillie grabbed Ginnie's arm and pulled her away from the others. "Check out your dad. Look how close he is to my mom. She knows about computers since she works on one all day."

Something in Tillie's tone made Ginnie protective of Dad. "My dad knows about computers too. He just doesn't see the point of getting a fancy new computer when the one we have does the job he needs it to do." Ginnie stopped short as a hurt look crossed Tillie's face.

"I just meant that your dad is really interested in what my mom is saying." Tillie pointed at their folks. "Look."

Toran moved to a different computer.

Miss Amanda played with a computer next to him and they asked each other questions about the models they were testing.

Dad took a step back and seemed to focus on Miss Amanda's face. His head tilted to the side and a smile lit his lips.

He likes her. He really does!

Ginnie turned to Tillie, who grinned even wider than when Dad teased about making Tillie her triplet. They fist-bumped, but Ginnie had to force herself to smile brightly, not sure why she wasn't happier with their success.

20

OSS IS DEFINITELY ON!

*W*hile Miss Amanda, Toran, and Dad discussed the benefits of RAM, speed, and graphics, Miss Amanda received a call on her cell phone. A happy smile perched on her lips as she hurried a couple aisles away. "Joe, how are you?"

Ginnie looked at Tillie. "Who is Joe?"

She shrugged. "Beats me."

Toran moved the mouse on a black laptop. "If I'm going to get a computer and spend that much money, I think I should go all the way and get what I *really* want, Dad."

"How much is it?"

"I'm still short almost two hundred, but it's already three hundred off the original price."

"That's a lot. You know how I feel about buying on credit." Dad shook his head sympathetically. "It'll be here when you have more money. You might even find a better deal."

"Not on this. I wouldn't ask, but this is an awesome sale. We'll be haying soon. I'll make two hundred easy. I'm good for it. Please, Dad?"

Dad looked uneasy. "It's not that I don't want to help, Tor, I do. I just don't want you thinking that what you want is only a loan or a credit card away. That's how people get in over their heads in a hurry." Dad scanned the other computers and pointed to the red one Toran had looked at earlier. "What about this one? The speed and memory are almost the same."

Toran shook his head. "But this one comes with extra programs right now. Look, a photo shop program, a great graphics card, and a $100 i-Tunes gift card."

"Tor, I know it's a great deal, but ..." Dad's words finished in a whisper.

Ginnie felt for her brother and oddly enough, for her dad.

Dad looked torn. He was a stickler for spending within their means and he seldom put limits on what they bought. If they wanted to buy a five pound bag of candy, he didn't argue if they had the money to pay cash. Dad looked like he wanted to bend, but Ginnie could tell he wouldn't.

"Toran, I have twenty-seven dollars if that'll help. And a gift card from Uncle Tom and Aunt Kate from my birthday." Ginnie pulled her wallet from her back pocket. "Maybe I could use the computer sometimes, for homework. Daddy, you could give him the cash and spend the gift card on whatever you want. He doesn't even have to pay me back."

"You can give him whatever you were going to give me as well. I don't care," Tillie offered.

Dad arched an eyebrow and smiled. "That's very generous of you girls. It makes me want to say 'yes', but there's still the principle. People should buy what they can actually afford. I don't want to set a different precedence here. That rule worked when I was a kid and it's worked for you guys. Two hundred dollars is not the same as a five dollar loan, Tor."

"But it's not two hundred dollars if I give him fifty-two." Ginnie smiled at Toran, happy to come to his rescue as he often did for her. "Then it's less than $150. And it's my money to give. Please, Daddy?"

Miss Amanda came back and scanned each face. "Why so glum?"

Toran shrugged, looked at Dad and blew out a slow breath. "Thanks anyway, Gin."

"Which one were you wanting the most, Toran?" Miss Amanda asked.

Toran pointed to the black laptop.

Miss Amanda read over the options card. "Well, my friend Joe can hook you up with this same model for a hundred and fifty dollars less. He's at the Member's Only club and was checking out something for me—so I asked him to check their computers."

"Toran only needs two dollars with my money," Ginnie hinted.

Dad's eyes brightened. "Since I have a membership there, I'll float him the other fifty. Ginnie and Tillie, you can keep your money. Amanda, I could hug you."

"Me first." Toran squeezed between them and hugged Miss Amanda tight. "Thanks so much!"

Miss Amanda smiled and hugged him back. "I'm glad I could help."

"Oh, you did. More than you know." Toran grinned at Dad. "Your turn." Toran took a step back and motioned Dad toward Miss Amanda.

Dad arched an eyebrow at Miss Amanda.

Miss Amanda nodded and stepped into his waiting arms. He held her tight. Dad winked at Ginnie, then rested his chin on the crown of Miss Amanda's head and seemed to relax. He lowered his voice to a whisper. "I owe you."

Miss Amanda's grin grew as wide as Tillie's had. She grabbed Ginnie's hand and pulled her away from their folks, squealing, 'E-e-e-e-e-e' under her breath.

21

THE RIDE HOME

*A*s they drove home from the computer store, Ginnie alternated between whispering happily with Tillie in the back seat of Dad's car and chatting with Toran about his computer, pushing away the occasional nagging feeling she couldn't explain.

Toran thanked Dad and Miss Amanda over and over as he browsed his owner's manual, exclaiming, "Guess what?" and "Check this out!"

"Toran, it was your money." Dad looked at him in the rear view mirror. "We just helped you out a little. Enjoy it, son."

"Oh, I will. I just can't believe I got such a cool computer." His mouth fell silent as his eyes scanned the manual.

Tillie giggled. "This is better than Christmas."

Ginnie nodded, pleased her brother was so happy.

And her dad.

And Miss Amanda.

And Tillie.

And herself.

But she couldn't seem to convince her belly to go along with the idea. Her insides twisted and turned like a mountain road. The bigger Dad's grin grew, the windier her tummy felt.

Turning her attention to Miss Amanda, she tried to describe her look.

What was that bonus word in spelling? Oh, yeah. Radiant.

Miss Amanda was definitely radiant. Her eyes shone and her face glowed. Ginnie sucked in a quick breath.

Miss Amanda has a crush on Daddy. She does. I know she does. On MY dad?

Ginnie shook her head and looked at him closely. Short, blond, curly hair. Dark blue eyes, nice smile.

He's an older version of Toran and the girls at school think Toran's cute, not that my science geek brother notices. I guess it makes sense that Miss Amanda thinks Daddy's cute, but still, he's... my... dad.

Ginnie leaned back and listened to the two of them talk about the pros and cons of apartment dwelling versus Miss Amanda buying a small home with a front yard. She elbowed Tillie and whispered. "Your mom is crushing on my dad."

Tillie studied both faces in the front seat. "OSS is s-o-o-o going to work out." They bumped fists.

Ginnie willed her doubts away. "I think so too. I'm glad I got to pick my sister."

"Me too." Tillie leaned toward Ginnie. "And *your dad* is crushing on *my mom.*"

Ginnie sat up stick straight, a wave of nausea rolling over her. *No, he is not. He can't.* The sparkle in his eye proved otherwise. *He was TOO crushing on Miss Amanda.* Dad turned down their dirt lane. A thought struck her as the tires crunched the gravel. If Mama were alive, she would be sitting where Miss Amanda was.

"Dad, you forgot Miss Amanda's car," Toran said.

Dad shrugged. "I didn't forget. I thought I'd drop you off to set up your computer. You seem like you're going to explode if you have to wait much longer to try out its bells and whistles." He tapped the steering wheel. "Look, there's Buzz with Uncle Ben on the front porch. If you have any trouble, Buzz will help you. Not that I think you'll need him."

Toran patted Dad's shoulder excitedly. "Ginnie's right. You're the best dad *ever*.

Dad stopped the car in his parking spot. "I try. Do you need some help?"

"No, I've got it." Toran opened his door. "Where are you going?"

"I thought I'd take these three lovely ladies out to dinner in their new outfits."

Ginnie glanced at the matching white T-shirts with flowing black vests that she and Tillie wore. Dad bought Ginnie one after Tillie picked hers out so they could match. She slid over to see Toran through the backseat window.

After Toran exited the car, Dad tousled his curls. "Since you're chomping at the bit to play with your new toy, I thought I'd put you out of your misery. Though you are welcome to join us."

"No thanks, Dad. I'm too excited to eat."

Dad chuckled. "That was my take on the situation." He leaned into the driver's seat and searched each face. "Feel free to get out and stretch your legs. Although I love my 'Best Dad' shirt, I thought I'd change into a dressier shirt to match you ladies. I'll only be a minute."

Tillie opened her door and snatched Ginnie's hand.

Ginnie had to scramble to keep up with her.

Dad disappeared into the house.

Miss Amanda joined Uncle Ben on the front porch swing after Buzz followed Toran inside.

Tillie pulled Ginnie over to the hammock. "What do you think about telling your dad we want to stay home and watch Toran set up his computer? He'll believe that, right?"

"I guess so."

"Cool. Then it's settled. We'll stay home."

Ginnie pasted a smile on her face to make Tillie happy. "We'll be missing out on a good dinner. Daddy doesn't like restaurants where you have to unwrap your food."

Tillie's laugh made her feel better. "Uncle Ben's the best cook ever. Even his leftovers are awesome. We'll survive." She pointed when

Dad entered the front porch dressed in a new button down royal blue shirt that matched his eyes. They walked over to the porch.

Ginnie didn't miss Dad's pleasant smile as he offered Miss Amanda his arm. Tillie leaned into her ear. "I think they want to be together. *Alone.* That's what we want too, isn't it?"

Is it? Ginnie couldn't help but notice that Miss Amanda's ecstatic smile mirrored Tillie's.

Her glance lingered on Dad's face. His features eased from content to truly happy. Dad's smile deepened when Miss Amanda entwined her arm in his.

I guess it is. Ginnie took a step back, peeking from Tillie's beaming face to Dad's focused gaze on Miss Amanda. Uncle Ben nodded his approval from the front porch swing.

Her winding mountain road feeling came back. The happy faces in front of her didn't lighten the storm brewing in her.

What about Mama?

Dad motioned toward the steps. "Are we ready, ladies?"

Tillie shook her head, her silly grin grew bigger. An even sillier giggle escaped. "No thanks. Ginnie and I want to stay here. But you two go and have fun."

Dad chuckled. "You guys are welcome to come."

Tillie shook Ginnie's arm. "Thanks, but no thanks. Right, Ginnie?"

"Oh yeah, right." Ginnie tugged her arm from Tillie's grasp, forcing herself to smile. "Have fun."

"If you're sure." He nodded at the swing. "Be good for Uncle Ben."

"Sure," Ginnie whispered.

"Yes, sir!" Tillie moved out of their way, grabbed her mom's hand, and practically pulled her along. "You two go have fun." She smiled even wider. "Lots of fun."

"We will ... if you don't make me fall down the stairs." Miss Amanda leaned over and kissed the top of Tillie's head. She squeezed Ginnie's hand. "Mind Uncle Ben, okay?"

Both nodded. Ginnie kept the smile plastered on her face. "Yes'm."

Waving, Dad rushed ahead of Miss Amanda to open her door.

"You're a true gentleman, Todd West," Miss Amanda cooed. She slid into her seat, her gaze never leaving Dad's until he closed her door.

"Aw shucks ma'am." Dad ducked his head, winked at Ginnie and Tillie, and jogged around the front of his car to the driver's side seat.

Ma'am? Ginnie's breath caught. *Sounds like Mama.*

She looked up, trying once again to recall the face that always eluded her. *Mama.* She gave a half-hearted wave as Dad and Miss Amanda backed down the hill.

22

THE JOURNALS

illie grabbed Ginnie's hands and happy-danced. Ginnie smiled for both of their sakes, and glanced at Uncle Ben, who sat on the swing. The rhythm of creaking chains and soft thud of his heels on the concrete porch soothed the growing panic Ginnie couldn't explain.

When Tillie slowed her jumping, Ginnie's smile brightened. "I forgot to put Calliope up. Why don't you see what Toran's doing? I'll see you soon."

"Okay. Are you going for a ride or just putting her up?"

Ginnie turned to Uncle Ben. "*Can* I go for a ride?"

"Make it quick. It'll be dark soon."

"I will. I haven't ridden her all day." Ginnie opened the screen door for Tillie. "I'll be back soon.

Tillie walked in. "Okay, have fun."

Ginnie turned to flee down the steps.

"Ginnie?"

She turned slowly toward her great-uncle. *Please don't want to talk. Please don't want to talk. Please don't want to talk.* "Yes?"

"Are you okay?" He lowered his voice to a whisper.

"Why wouldn't I be?"

"Don't answer my question with a question."

You do it all the time. Ginnie swallowed her frustration and forced a pleasant reply. "I'm fine. Can I go now?"

"Yes. But if you stop 'being fine' feel free to come see me."

"Yes, sir." Ginnie rushed down the stairs and turned, following the sidewalk along the side of the house until she reached the pasture. In a matter of minutes, she led Calliope through the gate.

Needing to get away quickly, she rode toward the back of their property where Uncle Ben couldn't see her riding bareback and without her helmet. Her dad would have a fit about not wearing her helmet. Ginnie pushed the guilt of disobedience away, then decided to ride Calliope up to the barn to get her helmet.

If Uncle Ben saw her without it and mentioned that to her dad, Daddy would ground her from Calliope. Not wanting to take a chance on losing her riding privileges, she turned Calliope toward the barn.

Ginnie slid off Calliope, waved away Uncle Jake's hunting dogs, Bandit and Rascal, who nipped at her heels.

She tied the reins to the barn door handle, jogged inside, and found her helmet. Ginnie fastened it as she hurried back to Calliope, untied her horse, and then led her to a bale of hay so that she could mount her. "The things I do for you, Calliope."

Calliope snorted, shaking her head.

Ginnie giggled, then stroked the mare's regal neck lovingly, her irritation at retrieving the helmet disappearing as she felt the velvety-soft hair glide under her palm. She turned Calliope toward the back pasture.

After reaching a pleasant pace, Ginnie cleared her mind and concentrated on the dream she often had when she rode. Mama sat behind her laughing, enveloping her in protective arms, with Mama's long blonde curls tickling her cheeks. The smell of a flowery perfume filled her senses and a feeling of peace coursed through her.

Today, the peaceful feeling eluded her as she considered why she wasn't happier about OSS working out.

Seeing Daddy truly happy with Miss Amanda was both welcoming and alarming.

I DO want Tillie to be my sister. We have a lot of fun together. And I love Miss Amanda. Why is it bugging me that Daddy seems to like her too? That's how OSS is supposed to work. They get married and Tillie moves in.

She forced her mind to clear, becoming one with Calliope. They skirted the outer edges of the growing corn, breathing in the smell of hot dirt and corn. The plants were only knee high, but the green sprouts grew thicker each day. The humidity finally dropped as the early evening wore on.

The sun would be out for another hour, but she wouldn't be allowed to ride much longer.

After deciding Calliope would benefit from a second lap, Ginnie thought about last month when Miss Amanda, Vi, Tillie, and herself had a 'girls' night out' together. They went to the mall and had a fun dinner where each picked food from a different country and shared with the others.

Miss Amanda offered them baklava, a Greek pastry with a honey glaze. She joked about not being a very good cook, but recognizing good cooking when she tasted it. She had complained good-naturedly that even though she helped Vi make fried chicken most every Sunday, hers never came out as good.

Tillie nodded her agreement.

Ginnie kicked her friend lightly under the table, not wanting Miss Amanda to feel bad. "That's not true. Your chicken is good."

Miss Amanda smiled. "You're a doll. And just for that, I'm going to treat you to one of my favorite indulgences." After dinner, she led them to two machines that looked like a cross between a tanning booth and a coffin. "Check this out." She patted one end of the open contraption. "Put your head here and lay on your tummy. The operator will put the lid down and these jets will squirt water up and down your body and give you a nice massage."

"But I didn't bring other clothes."

Vi laughed at that, making Ginnie angry.

Miss Amanda gave her a reassuring hug. "You won't need them.

The water stays in the plastic. Trust me, it feels lovely." Her soothing tone convinced Ginnie to try it.

Before taking off her shoes, Ginnie smirked at Vi. "Very funny. But I didn't know."

She put in the new earbuds she was offered, and lay down.

The operator plugged the earbuds in and started the machine. Soft music played while warm, water-powered jets pulsed over her feet, tingling them. Soon, she relaxed. The jets crept up her legs and back, smoothing away tension and inviting the 'lovely' experience Miss Amanda had mentioned. It was over too quickly, but she was glad she had trusted Miss Amanda, who promised to bring her again.

A warm blast of air turned her attention back to the present and Calliope. They were almost back to where they started.

Sighing, she turned her mare and they walked slowly back to the barn where she dismounted and led Calliope to her horse wash rack. She talked with her mare as she applied the horse's shampoo and then rinsed her off. She let Calliope drip while she located the sweat scraper to squeegee the water off. "Thanks, Girl, I needed the ride."

Calliope nudged Ginnie affectionately.

"I'm glad you understand 'people,' I wish I understood 'horse' better." Ginnie offered her mare several slices of an apple, then led her back to her stall, freshened her water, picked up Calliope's brush and stroked her back.

A sparrow flew around the barn. "He's lost, huh, Calliope?" Ginnie took her time brushing her equine friend, each stroke brightening her mood.

Finally, she couldn't delay any longer. She offered Calliope fresh hay, kissed her forelock, and put the brush away. "See you tomorrow."

After latching the stall gate, Ginnie turned, hearing soft meowing. She glanced around the barn, but didn't see any of their cats.

"Meow."

"Hey, Princess, where are you?"

"Mee-ooow. Meow."

A piece of straw drifted down from the loft. Ginnie looked up, a quick splash of gray disappearing above her. "Are you hiding your babies?" Ginnie listened hard, but didn't hear any further mewing. She climbed the ladder, but didn't see any sign of Princess. "Here, kitty, kitty."

On her way to investigate some rustling of hay in the corner, she heard the soft mews of Princess's babies. One, two, three, four, five. All there, and all alive. "Hey Princess. Why'd you move them to this barn?" She lightly stroked each soft body. "You need your mama, don't you? I know the feeling."

Her gaze darted around the loft and a flash of movement drew her toward the back of the loft where unfamiliar bulges and bumps were stacked. As she came closer, she made out boxes and more blanket draped bundles.

Squinting, she read Dad's handwriting on some of the boxes. *Baby girl clothes, 0-6 months, Kitchen stuff, Toran's toys, Ginnie's dresses, Pageant Costumes, Trophies, Q's Journals, G & T's Scrapbooks, Q's clothes,* among others.

She coughed when she breathed in dust while lifting a blanket that covered a wood desk.

Under the desk, she found a box marked *Q's Journals.* It was a medium-sized box with books of varying sizes and colors. On top lay a blue-and-pink-striped journal titled "My Pregnancy Journal." The stripes caught her eye. She opened the book to the first entry.

I surprised Todd with the news that we're expecting a baby! He was so happy! The baby is due the second week of June. In a couple of weeks, I'll go to the doctor's and be able to hear the baby's heartbeat. I just can't get over how our love for each other has turned into a real live person. What a miracle. We're both dancing on the ceiling!

Hey! She's talking about me and Toran. Ginnie's hand flew to her mouth. *I'll bet she's surprised when she finds out there's two of us! Oh my goodness! MAMA is writing this!*

Ginnie stumbled, excitement pulsing through her. *I can't believe it. Mama .... wrote ... this.*

"Awesome sauce!" Ginnie scanned the next couple pages, almost dropping the journal as she realized the treasure she'd found.

A few entries later, Mama wrote of going to her doctor's appointment to hear the heartbeat. It sounded strange to the doctor, so she ordered a sonogram and found not one, but two babies.

Their hearts beat so close in rhythm that one seemed to echo the other, rather than be two distinct heartbeats.

Mama wrote:

"I was so glad Todd went with me today! I'm not sure he would have believed me otherwise. It was so exciting to see our tiny babies. Todd's sure we are going to have one boy and one girl. I'm betting on two boys. West men don't seem to know how to make girls! 😊

Ginnie laughed at the smiley face Mama had drawn.

Of the 12 cousins in Todd's generation, Vi's the only girl. Vi is s-o-o-o excited at the prospect of two babies. Aunt Sadie has started on a second quilt. She finished the first one already! Aunt Sadie has never seen a picture of a sonogram before, so she was super excited to see sonogram photos with TWO babies. I will invite her to another sonogram. I can't imagine ever growing tired of looking at our little miracles!"

The ruffle of bird's feathers startled Ginnie.

Panic surged. Not sure how much time had passed. She decided to bring the box of journals to her room.

It took some juggling to get it down the ladder, but she managed to carry the whole box. After adjusting the weight, she walked to the front of the barn, peeking in all directions in case someone appeared.

She darted down the hill and made her way into the side porch, leaving the box on the washing machine while she peeked in the kitchen. She heard Uncle Jake joking in the dining room. He was sitting at the table with Vi, and Uncle Ben, playing "Can't Stop."

Quietly, she crossed the kitchen, and let out a breath. *All clear.* She opened the door next to the kitchen sink that hid stairs which led to the second story.

She tiptoed back to the side porch and snatched up the box. Glancing each way, she waited until she heard the roll of dice and good-natured banter before hurrying to the stairs. She closed the door. Dark enveloped her. After fumbling with the light switch, she crept quietly up the wooden stairs, grimacing when they creaked.

Nobody can hear me. Her heart pounded in her ears. *I'm not doing anything wrong.*

When she reached the top, she opened the door leading to the room where they stored their food neatly on shelves. It always reminded her of a mini-mart. Rows and rows of canned goods and paper products arranged neatly. They never worried when foul weather hit, anything the family needed could be found somewhere in this room. She turned off the light and crept to the other door that opened into Vi's room. Her heart raced. She reminded herself that Vi was in the dining room.

Sugar beets! I have to go through Toran's room to get to mine. Tillie and Toran are in Toran's room!

She retraced her steps to the food room and searched for a place to hide the box. After debating with herself about what to do, she finally pulled out the striped journal and stuck it in the back of her jeans and tucked her t-shirt over it.

She hid the box on a shelf behind some blankets.

Disappointed, she whispered. "I'll be back for you soon."

Ginnie leaned against Vi's door. Hearing nothing, she opened the door a crack and let out a quiet breath. The door creaked as she opened it wider. "Shhh!" she hissed, darting into the hallway.

She came to a sudden stop, bumping into her cousin, Buzz.

23

HIDING THE JOURNALS

*B*uzz cleared his throat, arching an eyebrow. "Hey Gin, why are you in Vi's room?"

Turning so he didn't see the heat rising to her cheeks, Ginnie struggled to regain her composure. She slid her palm down her jeans. "I-I just came up the back way. Through the food room."

"You probably shouldn't do that." He took a step forward, peeked around Vi's room, and then pulled the door shut.

"I only came through Vi's room to save time. I didn't *stay* in there."

He frowned. "Why do you look like you were doing something you shouldn't?"

"I didn't do anything wrong."

"Who are you trying to convince, me or you?"

Ginnie crossed her arms and glared. "I'm telling the truth."

Just like Uncle Ben and Dad, Buzz had an annoying 'scary quiet' voice he used when he took control of a conversation.

Unlike Uncle Ben, Ginnie wasn't afraid to stand up to him. She pointed at the staircase in front of her. "I'll use these steps from now on." She took a step forward, which he blocked with a counter-step, his blue-gray eyes appraising her.

She studied her cousin, so much like his dad. Normally they coexisted pleasantly enough, not seeing much of each other with Buzz juggling a full time job, college classes, his chores, and a girlfriend. Toran and Buzz spent a lot of time together, each being avid book-worms and science geeks, but Ginnie didn't have much in common with Buzz.

"Hey, Buzz, can you help me with something?" Toran asked from his doorway. "Hi, Gin."

Buzz took a step backward, his eyes never leaving Ginnie's face. "Sure. Be right there."

"I told Tillie I'd be right back. Gotta go." Ginnie side-stepped around Buzz, and hurried to Toran. She slipped past her brother and smiled when Tillie pointed at Toran's computer screen. "That's cool. Gotta change. Back in a minute." She continued to her room, shutting the door behind her.

Glancing around, she rejected the idea of hiding Mama's journal in a dresser or desk drawer. She walked over to her bed and slid it under her pillow. After fluffing her pillows, she took a calming breath and let it out slowly.

"Chillax. You're not doing anything wrong." Even though she whispered the words in the most confident voice she could muster, Ginnie couldn't shake the feeling that Dad would disagree. "Well, he's not here and Mama wrote the journal about me ... and Toran."

Instead of debating with herself about whether or not she'd share her find with Toran, she pushed the matter aside, preferring to focus on which shirt she should change into.

With one last glance at her bed, and a soft sigh, she reached for the doorknob, and forced a pleasant smile to her lips. She might as well try and enjoy Tillie and Toran's company until Dad and Miss Amanda returned from their date.

When Miss Amanda took Tillie home, she could ditch the family and enjoy Mama's journals all by herself.

24

THEY'RE BA-A-A-A-ACK

*W*hen the familiar sound of gravel crunched, Ginnie looked up from the rainbow she was drawing in chalk on the sidewalk in front of the farmhouse.

"They're back," Tillie squealed, leaping up and wiping her hands on her jeans. Ginnie dropped her piece of green chalk and jumped to her feet, waiting for Dad to pull into his parking spot. Miss Amanda parked behind him.

Daddy must have dropped her off at the go-kart place to pick up her car.

Tillie rushed to her mom and hugged her.

Dad put his hands up in a 'stop' motion when Ginnie approached him. "I'm always in for a hug, honey, but this is my new shirt."

Ginnie glanced down at her own shirt and forearms, which were covered in green, purple, and bright pink chalk. She giggled. "Sorry."

"Don't be." Dad leaned over and kissed the top of her head. "You look like you had fun. I just don't want your fun all over my shirt. I'm glad you changed out of your new clothes."

"We did have fun." Ginnie smiled at Miss Amanda. "Where'd you guys go?"

"Rosalia's. A nice Italian place with the most amazing chicken fettuccini Alfredo. We'll take you girls and Toran sometime. They have the best Italian bread with seasonings. Mmmm."

"Sounds yummy." Tillie licked her lips.

Ginnie turned to Dad. She was glad he and Miss Amanda had a good time together. Ginnie *wanted* them to have a good time. But right now, even more, she just wanted to be with him. An hour of talking about the success of OSS while making chalk drawings was enough.

Tillie had pointed out all the benefits of OSS to her. They could be together all the time. Their parents would be happier. Even Toran had seemed to like the idea.

After all, he got Dad and Miss Amanda to hug ... and Toran didn't even know about OSS. Ginnie's room was big enough for two beds, not that they needed two because her full-size bed had always been big enough for her and Tillie. Even Dad's car was the right size for their new family.

Ginnie also had the journals to consider. Now that she had Mama to herself, maybe Mama would give her some insight on what to think or feel.

Catching her eye, Tillie raised her brows in question.

Ginnie shrugged, giving a slight shake of her head. She didn't want to ask Tillie to spend the night. She turned to Dad. "We have church tomorrow. Any idea when Uncle Jake'll get home?"

Dad looked at his watch. "Sometime before midnight. Gin, you should get a shower. Tillie, why don't you get your new shirt and you two can be twins at church tomorrow ... or not."

Tillie nodded. "Thanks again. I love it."

"You're very welcome." He smiled at Tillie as she walked past him. Dad motioned for Ginnie to follow Tillie, then turned to Miss Amanda.

She reached a hand out to him. He took it and then stopped, glancing at Ginnie. He nodded at the front porch.

He looks ... embarrassed. Why? Oh, because I'm watching.

Dad nodded again for Ginnie to keep going. She did, but paused at the front door. Her dad kissed Miss Amanda's hand and drew her into a quick hug. Miss Amanda giggled, like the girls at school when a boy they liked waved at them.

But he's ... my ... dad. Ginnie shook her head, trying to calm her racing heart, and followed Tillie upstairs.

25

READING THE JOURNAL

*T*he warmth of the shower soothed Ginnie's anxiety about OSS and helped wash away the guilt she felt about hogging Mama's journals to herself.

The next few entries dealt with Mama's pregnancy changes: her nausea and her cravings–waffles with cherry pie filling on top, double hot fudge sundaes, and peas in cheese sauce.

The worst part about being pregnant (besides the stretch marks, the nausea, and being tired all the time) is not being able to ride Love. Vi's happy to exercise her for me, but I miss being on her. We have spent very few days apart in the last seven years.

Todd won't admit it, but I think he's glad I can't spend as much time with her as I usually do. I tease him about being jealous of my horse, but he doesn't think it's funny when I remind him that Eternal Love was in my life first.

Sometimes I wish he could be pregnant instead of me, but then I think about the babies growing inside me and I wouldn't have it any other way. Todd's a lot more patient with my moods than I could ever be if we switched places. He never complains when I have a craving and does his best to get me what I want. He's definitely a keeper.

Imagining her six-foot, two-inch dad with a pregnant belly, made Ginnie giggle. Reading how he treated Mama—and how much Mama appreciated his kindness—bubbled warm feelings for each of her parents. Ginnie continued to read how Daddy surprised Mama with fun gifts of odd food, new hair barrettes, or nice smelling lotion he applied to her aching back.

Ginnie squealed when she came to an entry about the sonogram that would tell the sexes of the babies. Then she giggled when she reminded herself that she already knew the outcome.

Todd's still sure we're having one of each. I think he's wrong, so I agreed he could name the girl "Eliza" after his mom and I'd name the boy. I still think we're going to have Cody and Jared, but we'll find out tomorrow.

Ginnie continued to read about the preparations Mama made for their birth, when she heard a knock at her door. Jumping, she called out. "Uh, just a second!" She shoved the book under her covers and tried to look innocent. "Come in."

Dad opened the door. "Hi, honey. Are you ready for bed?"

"Yes. Did you have fun with Miss Amanda?"

His smile widened as he crossed the room. He pulled the covers up snug around her chin. "I did. I just wanted to say good-night and see how things are with you."

"I'm tired. I rode Calliope and gave her a good rub down."

"I won't keep you then. Pleasant dreams."

"We can talk if you want," she said a little too quickly.

He stopped. "What do you want to talk about?"

Ginnie tapped her finger on her cheek. "You going out with Miss

Amanda made me think about your first date with Mama. Where did you take *her*?"

The alarm in his eyes made Ginnie almost regret asking.

"Um." He turned slightly away. "Nothing as fancy. We had Bar-B-Q sandwiches at the rodeo." He kissed her forehead. "Night, honey."

"Night, Daddy." He beat a hasty retreat out her door, switching off her light. *Great.* Ginnie sighed. *He never wants to talk about Mama.*

26

CHURCH

Ginnie sat between Uncle Jake and Dad during church; surprised to see how many times Dad looked toward Miss Amanda. She was equally surprised at how many times Miss Amanda returned the sneaking glances. Occasionally their eyes would meet and their smiles would grow bigger.

When Ginnie nudged Dad, like Dad did to her when she didn't pay attention to the speaker, he alternated between seeming embarrassed and acting irritated.

He finally faced forward and made sure she did too.

Uncle Jake leaned over Ginnie to whisper "Busted!" in Dad's ear.

"Knock it off." He threw Uncle Jake a disgusted look and softened it only a little for Ginnie's benefit.

"I think your old man got bit ... by the lo-o-o-ve bug," Uncle Jake whispered in Ginnie's ear.

Ginnie's belly tightened. She elbowed Uncle Jake and scolded. "You need to be reverent."

He pursed his lips into a pout. "Hey, I'm just letting you know your plan worked. Geez, Trouble."

Panic gripped her. *Uncle Jake knows about OSS?* She peeked at

Dad. *Does Daddy know? HOW could he know?* She and Tillie had been so careful.

Ginnie glanced from Uncle Jake to Dad.

"What?" Dad asked quietly.

"Nothing." Ginnie shrugged and glared at Uncle Jake.

He leaned to her ear. "Why are you looking like you just got weaned on a sour pickle?"

She pushed up against him with her shoulder. "We're supposed to be quiet."

"What's with you?"

Ginnie crossed her arms and looked straight ahead.

Uncle Jake tried again. "Lighten up. You don't want your face to freeze like that." His whisper tickled her ear. She rubbed her ear and stood, stepping in front of Dad.

Dad frowned.

"Uncle Jake's buggin' me."

Uncle Jake's mouth dropped open.

Dad scooted toward his brother and made room for Ginnie, between himself and Toran. Ginnie threw Uncle Jake a satisfied smirk and sat next to her brother.

Uncle Ben raised a questioning brow.

Ginnie looked as innocent as she could and pointed at Uncle Jake. Uncle Ben gave a knowing nod and frowned at Uncle Jake.

Ginnie could hardly hold back a laugh when Uncle Jake threw her a look that clearly said 'traitor.'

Usually she teased with him about her dad all the time, but today was different.

They were in church after all.

And who's the traitor? How does he know about OSS? And what *does he know?*

A strange thought crossed Ginnie's mind. *Did Tillie tell him? She might, but not without telling me first. Or would she?*

27

INVITING THE CHANDLERS OVER

When Sunday School was over, Ginnie darted out of class. She didn't know how to deal with her mixed-up feelings and seeing Tillie miserable made her feel even worse. Scanning the hallways, she searched for either an escape or an excuse, hoping to provide a distraction for her growing nausea.

Hurting Tillie's feelings wasn't going over well.

After rounding a corner, she spied Dad and Miss Amanda talking with Austin's parents.

Yes! I just need to get Vi or Uncle Ben to say it's okay to invite the Chandler's over for lunch.

She turned and found Uncle Ben coming out of a classroom and asked him. "Sure, Gin. We haven't had Pete and Lauren over in ages. It'll be fun to visit."

"Thanks, Uncle Ben. I'll tell them."

Uncle Jake and Vi had joined the group by the time Ginnie arrived. "Uncle Ben says to come over for lunch. Can Austin bring Traxx, please?"

"Is Uncle Ben cooking?" Austin's mom smiled and adjusted her book bag. "If so, I'm in."

Uncle Jake laughed. "No. *I* drew the short stick—but I'm barbequing—ribs and chicken. You can help me, Pete."

Austin's dad reached his hand to Uncle Jake's. "Count me in, Jake."

"Cool, I'll tell Austin," Ginnie squealed.

"And your brother and Tillie? Where are they?" Dad glanced down the hallway. "You four are usually stuck together like glue."

Ginnie shrugged.

No way was she offering an explanation.

28

ANNIE OAKLEY

*W*ith a bit of careful maneuvering, Ginnie secured a ride home with Austin and his folks, to avoid Tillie. She decided if Tillie asked why she was acting weird, she'd blame it on being tired. After all, she had stayed up late reading the journal.

Ginnie sat back in the mini-van and stared out the window, thinking about an entry she had read several times the night before.

Her dad had come home early from work and snuck in their master bedroom window with a bouquet of roses. After scattering some petals on their bed, he changed into some satin pajamas Mama had bought for him. With soft music playing, he waited on their bed, tossing marbles one at a time at the bedroom door, wanting her to come investigate.

The first time Ginnie read it, she was shocked that her dad had a romantic side. As far as she knew, he'd never been on a date, at least since Mama died. Of course, they must've dated before they got married, but she'd never really thought about *that*.

After reading the whole entry a few times, it got less weird thinking of her parents like the kids at school sneaking kisses in the hallway. Ginnie had giggled quite a bit when she read her favorite part of the journal entry:

.   .   .

I found him all right, after I kicked the door open and threatened to venti-late him if he didn't get out. It took a few seconds to figure out that it was my husband in our bedroom and not some low-life with bad intentions. The surprised look on his face was priceless. Todd reminded me of a cartoon character with his eyes practically popping out of their sockets. He raised his hands and said, "Whoa, Annie Oakley, I come in peace."

I spun the gun a couple of times and then pretended to slide it into an imaginary holster, relieved he wasn't a crazy stalker or drug addict hoping for an easy score. It took all I had to keep a straight face as I bartered with him. "I got half a mind to make you dance, Blondie. Or you can buy me a double fudge sundae, your choice."

That was a no-brainer; we went for sundaes. I should have asked for a pedicure, complete with a foot massage. I realize now he got off wa-a-a-ay too easy. On the way to the ice cream shop I started thinking about what could have happened and then I got mad, and yelled at him for scaring me. He apologized, but couldn't stop smiling. GRRR!

Ginnie giggled, imagining her usually calm dad trying to reason with her crazy, angry mother.

Mama had felt so bad she talked to Aunt Sadie about it.

Aunt Sadie was VERY sympathetic when I told her how badly my hands shook when I realized how close I'd come to half-orphaning my unborn children and making myself a widow. She felt for Todd as well, but agreed he should've come through the front door like a normal husband. Vi took Todd's side and thought he acted very romantically. Maybe so, but he KNEW I had a gun—and he and Jake made sure I knew how to use it. WHAT DID HE EXPECT?

.   .   .

Yeah, what? Ginnie laughed, wanting to hurry home to read the incident again.

"What's so funny?" Austin asked.

Ginnie clamped her mouth shut and looked around the Chandler's mini-van. Austin and his mom both looked at her expectantly. "Uh, nothing. Sorry, you were saying?"

Austin shook his head. "I didn't say anything. You just started laughing."

Ginnie considered telling him about the journals, but decided against it.

Miss Lauren shifted in her seat to see Ginnie better. "What was so funny, Gin?"

"Nothing." Her face heated. "I heard a funny joke, but now that I think about it, it's not so funny." They turned down the lane.

Ginnie sat back in her seat, welcoming the distraction of the crunching gravel.

29

NEANDERTHAL CLUB

By hanging out with Austin and Toran, Ginnie avoided being alone with Tillie, but made an extra effort to be nice to her, hoping Tillie would forget how rudely she'd behaved at church. She was counting on Tillie being her loyal and forgiving self.

After lunch, The Four Musketeers settled into their normal routine, enjoying the barbequed ribs and chicken that Uncle Jake cooked. Each piled their plates with salads and corn-on-the-cob as well. Before long, Ginnie and Tillie reached an unspoken agreement to forgive and forget. They exchanged sympathetic smiles and then relieved hugs.

Austin was oblivious to the tension, but Toran raised a questioning brow. Ginnie shook her head and squeezed Tillie's hand in a friendly way. After lunch, they all ended up more or less in the kitchen, putting up dirty dishes.

"I'll help with the dishes," Dad offered.

But Vi wouldn't hear of it. She pushed Dad and Miss Amanda toward the side porch door. "Off with you two. We can handle things. Take Todd and go for a walk, Amanda. No Neanderthals allowed."

"I'm volunteering to help, so how can I be a Neanderthal?" Dad protested. "That makes me enlightened, not a caveman."

"You know you'd rather take a walk. Off you go." Vi motioned him to the side porch door.

Miss Amanda blushed, as she nodded toward Tillie and Ginnie. "Vi-i-i."

Ginnie giggled at her discomfort and then glanced at Dad.

He was trying not to laugh as he held his hand out to Miss Amanda. "Fine, but I offered." Dad bowed to the group. "Ladies ..." Smiling, they headed for the door.

Tillie ran ahead of them and opened the screen door. "Have fun."

Something about her dad's smile smoothed the uneasiness Ginnie felt earlier when she watched him and Miss Amanda sneaking glances at church.

A warm, comfortable feeling swept over her.

After the screen door banged shut, Vi rolled her eyes again, teasing, "I thought they'd never leave. Some people need a literal push to get things going."

Tillie swished her towel at Vi and laughed. "So, when are you and *Preston* getting married?"

"That's a good question, Vi. What's the hold-up?" Miss Lauren asked.

Vi smirked at Tillie. "My cousins, Jake and Todd. The boneheads are playing their Neanderthal game and psyching Preston out."

Vi dropped a handful of forks in the dishwater, splashing Ginnie. "Jake took Preston out target shooting a couple weeks ago. Since he's a hunter and was a marksman in the army, he showed Preston up close and personal what happens to a watermelon roughly the size of a human head on a fence post at a hundred and fifty yards when it's shot with a double ought six rifle. It wasn't pretty."

"He wanted Preston to know just how far he could 'reach out and touch someone,' eh?" Miss Lauren joked.

Ginnie and Tillie burst out laughing.

Vi wagged a scolding finger. "You think it's funny now, but wait until you two turn sixteen and want to go on your first dates. Trust me, they're planning worse for you guys." Vi added another plate to the rack. "Jake actually lies awake at night thinking up ways to intimidate my dates."

Tillie giggled harder.

"He did the same thing to a couple of Amanda's boyfriends as well." Vi shook her head. "I hope Amanda and Todd work out. She says he's great as a date. He'd better be, because he's not so much fun as a big brother. At least when it comes to *me* dating. He's almost as bad as Jake and now they've got Buzz starting. And he's my *little* brother."

Tillie elbowed Ginnie and mouthed, "OSS is working."

Ginnie nodded. Relief swept over her when she realized Tillie had completely forgiven her.

OSS was still on. And it felt completely right for the first time since they started scheming.

Miss Lauren swiveled toward Vi. "The guys are just looking out for you, when they tease Preston. Besides, Preston's been around for two years. It's Preston's move. *When is he going to get around to asking you to marry him?*"

Vi shook her head, looked around the dining room, and toward the hallway to see if anyone could hear them. "Preston asked me to marry him last night."

Tillie jumped up and down. "E-e-e-e!"

Vi shushed her. "He hasn't asked Dad for permission yet. He's still planning that one."

Ginnie laughed and put a dry glass in the cupboard.

Miss Lauren dropped the washrag on the counter and hugged Vi. "Violet West! You better spill! And I mean *now*. How did he propose? And where's the ring?"

"He has it. It's gorgeous, but I wanted him to give it to me after my dad says yes." Vi leaned against the counter and dried her hands on a towel. "Preston did the sweetest thing! He put a satin blindfold on me and walked me through the park. And then he stopped me in front of a footbridge and told me to wait. I listened to him walk across the bridge. After a couple of minutes, he called to me to take off the blind fold, so I did. He was holding up a sign that said 'I kissed the ground you walked on. Will you marry me?' I looked down and there were foil wrapped chocolate lips all across the bridge."

"That is s-o-o-o-o sweet!" Tillie squealed.

Vi nodded. "The only thing that would make this more perfect is if my mom were here."

Sadness spiked through Ginnie when she caught the wistful look in her cousin's eyes.

Aunt Sadie's gonna miss Vi's wedding and ... Mama's gonna miss mine.

30

SUNDAY SCHOOL

*W*hen Ginnie reached her Sunday school classroom, she scanned the ten seats arranged in a "U." Austin sat in one of the seats at the top of the "U." She glanced out the door behind her. Tillie and Toran were walking down the hall, about thirty seconds away.

"Scoot down one, Austin."

He looked puzzled, but moved anyway.

Ginnie sat in the seat he vacated. "Hey, we need to race the horses, I think Calliope misses Traxx."

"We should." He peeked at the door and patted the chair on his other side. "Tor, I saved you a spot."

Ginnie smiled at her brother and Tillie, then turned back to Austin. "Hey, I think Uncle Jake's barbequing after church. I'll ask if your whole family can come."

"Cool, I want to see Toran's computer." Austin twisted to face her brother. "It sounds sweet."

"It's the sweetest," Toran agreed.

Ginnie refused to make eye contact with Tillie, who sat in the seat next to Toran.

Their teacher came in and shushed the class.

Ginnie glued her eyes on the teacher the whole period, pretending to be interested in his lesson on making good choices.

She was irritated with Tillie, but couldn't figure out why.

With Austin and Toran acting as human shields, Ginnie explored why she was being so weird. Maybe because OSS worked quicker than she thought it would. It had been fun plotting and scheming, and that part of OSS seemed to be over.

Maybe I don't really want a new sister.

She sucked in a breath and glanced at Tillie. She couldn't figure out if Tillie looked puzzled or hurt.

Her thoughts traveled back to the day she had met Tillie in kindergarten. They sat across the table from each other at lunch time. A little boy named Stevie sat next to Tillie and knocked over her carton of milk. He didn't apologize and Tillie burst into tears.

Stevie laughed and pointed at Tillie. "You're a crybaby. Quit crying, you baby."

Fury had bubbled through her. Lucky for Stevie, Ginnie remembered the 'no hitting' rule just in time. Instead, she stepped up on the bench, picked up Tillie's milk, leaned on the table and poured the rest of it over Stevie's head.

Then crossed her arms, satisfied with her revenge.

"Hey!" he had protested and started bawling.

Ginnie smirked. "Who's the crybaby now?"

She had to spend the rest of lunch in timeout, but she didn't care. Tillie and she were inseparable after that.

31

THE PROPOSAL

*G*innie cheered up quickly when family and friends gathered together in the family room. The adults sat on the dark plum leather couch and loveseat with Ginnie and Tillie making room in front of their green brick fireplace.

After pacing near the doorway, Preston finally got up the nerve to approach Uncle Ben, who sat in his favorite moss green armchair.

Preston started out quiet, but the more he talked, the more confident he became. "I would be so honored if you'd allow me the privilege of marrying your daughter." He paused, his eyes never once leaving Uncle Ben's face.

Uncle Ben rubbed his chin and gave a good show of considering the matter.

Tillie tugged Ginnie's T-shirt sleeve and smiled. They sat on the floor near the hearth, waiting quietly with everyone else.

The silence beat loudly in their ears.

"Daddy! Just say 'yes' already," Vi insisted, snatching Preston's hand.

Tillie giggled next to Ginnie.

Uncle Ben stood. "Now, Violet, I do believe the question was directed at *me*." He put his thumb gently on her cheek and smiled. "This is the man you want at your side for all times?"

Vi nodded, her auburn waves covering his hand.

"Very well." Uncle Ben turned to Preston. "If you promise to continue to treat her well and keep this light shining in her eyes, I can see my way to trusting you with *my one and only daughter, the joy of her mother's and my hearts.*"

His words were warm, but Ginnie knew Preston didn't miss the warning they bore. She stifled a giggle as Preston swallowed hard and nodded. "Yes sir, I intend to do everything in my power to make her happy."

Uncle Ben held out his hand. "That's all I ask."

Preston's eyes widened. When he realized that Uncle Ben had granted his request, he took Uncle Ben's hand in his and pumped it, grinning the biggest grin Ginnie had ever seen on his face.

Uncle Ben drew him into a bear hug. "And what took you so long to ask? I thought I'd be rocking in an old folks' home before you got around to asking me."

The whole room erupted in laughter.

Preston glared at Uncle Jake, who stood beside him, laughing while offering a welcoming handshake.

Dad raised his eyebrows and grinned while Miss Amanda giggled softly. They exchanged a quick kiss before joining Buzz, Toran, Tillie, and Austin's family crowding around the happy couple.

Ginnie hung back a minute before she joined the throng.

Even though she teased Vi alot about marrying Preston and moving out, a pit grew in her stomach at the thought, making her feel like a hollowed out chocolate Easter Bunny.

32

THE WALK

*A*fter their friends left, Ginnie started upstairs to escape to the quiet of her room and Mama's journal. Dad opened the screen door. "Gin, there you are. Come here for a minute, please."

Trying not to groan, Ginnie took a breath and turned toward him. "Yes?" *Does he know I have the journals?*

"Please take a walk with me."

Ginnie searched his face. A request to take a walk either meant: 1) She was in very big trouble, or 2) He was worried about her or something that had to do with her. Or sometimes it could mean, 3) He wanted clarification about something, but that usually resulted in adjustment to a punishment he was considering, sometimes in her favor, and sometimes not.

Today he didn't seem angry, but she couldn't be sure this walk wouldn't come without a lecture. After dodging her apology to Tillie all day, she didn't want to spend intense alone time with her dad, who had an unnerving way of getting her to spill her guts when she didn't want to.

She scanned her brain for an acceptable answer to ditch him and came up with a big fat zero.

When he arched an eyebrow and tightened his jaw, Ginnie knew she waited too long to respond. She forced a smile and took a step toward him. "Sure, Daddy."

If she couldn't avoid him, she might as well soften him up.

His jaw relaxed, but his eyes narrowed with suspicion.

She flashed him her best smile and hurried down the remaining five steps. When she reached the grass, Ginnie looked at him for a clue as to where they would walk.

Straight ahead down the lane was usually better than up the hill toward the barn.

He nodded straight ahead.

She blew out a relieved breath.

Whew! He just wants to visit.

Dad must have realized her concern. Once they passed by his green sedan and Vi's purple convertible VW bug, he laid a gentle hand on her shoulder. "You're not in trouble. I just need you to clarify something for me."

A sick feeling bubbled inside her. "About what?"

He stopped walking, hooked his thumbs in his front jean pockets, and smiled. "Could you please quit looking like you're gonna puke? I promise, you're not in trouble." Dad winked and then let his tone turn a little more serious. "Unless you're hiding something that is worthy of punishment, then I take back that promise and reserve the right to make a new judgment based on the new information."

He crossed his arms and wiggled his eyebrows. "*Is* there something I should know?"

Ginnie measured his words and searched his face. *The journals?* He seemed only a little concerned she might be hiding something. She shook her head. "No, sir."

He hugged her. "Good. I wanted to make this quick."

They walked together down the lane a few more yards before he spoke again. *For someone who wants to 'make this quick', you sure are taking your sweet time.*

"Correct me if I'm wrong, but there seemed to be a lot of activities planned this week where both Miss Amanda and Tillie were involved ... and me."

She avoided Dad's eyes and stared at the alfalfa growing on the other side of the brook.

"I'll take your silence as that was the intention."

Ginnie swallowed, but didn't answer.

Tillie's gonna freak if he messes up our plans.

"You seemed happy that Amanda and I started talking more." Dad tilted her chin and looked her straight in the eye.

"Kinda."

"Kinda?"

"Yes?" Ginnie's gaze dropped to his cowboy boots.

"Which is it? Kinda or yes?"

"Both."

He shook his head like he was trying to clear an Etch-A-Sketch. "Care to expound on your answer?"

"Do I have to?"

"I'd appreciate it."

Ginnie's heart beat quicker.

Her thoughts tumbled in her head, making no sense at all. She glanced at him. He had on his 'patient' face. He'd wait however long it took for her to explain.

Explain what? That she had wanted a sister—and then she didn't— and now she did again?

That seeing her dad and her best friend's mom crushing on each other didn't feel like she thought it would? That the only mom she ever knew was getting married and would probably be around even less than she already was?

She let out a sigh, shrugged, and then turned away from him. *Getting a sister is getting too complicated.*

He snapped his fingers. "I get it now."

She jerked her head toward him. "Get what?"

"What happened." He nodded faster. "I get it now."

"What are you talking about?" Her throat went dry.

"Your little scheme to get a new mom. Too much reality when I went along with it."

Ginnie's mouth dropped open. "Huh?"

His eyes danced. She was sure he no longer saw her as he continued to nod. "That's it."

She stepped back. "A new mom? Are you crazy?" Ginnie's hands flew to her hips. "I don't need a mom, *I. Have. Vi.*"

Ginnie whirled away from him, anger and disbelief exploding as quickly as the baking soda and vinegar in her science project volcano. "I don't want a *new* mom, I want *my* mom."

33

WHO NEEDS A NEW MOM?

scheme for a new mom? Was he absolutely nuts?
Ginnie fisted and unfisted her hands and then bolted down the lane, toward the main road.

"Hey!" Dad's surprised voice followed first and then his boots crunched behind her, every step coming closer.

She ran faster.

"Ginnie, wait up."

How could he think that? He doesn't know me at all.

Adrenaline surged through her. Her shoes seemed to have strapped on rockets. She kept running.

His boots thundered behind her. "Virginia Mae Stratton West! I said stop!" He grabbed her arm and pulled her backward, then balanced her when she stumbled. He steeled his eyes on hers, angry sparks practically shooting from the dark blue spheres. "What was that all about?"

Ginnie refused to look at him, focusing instead on the growing corn behind him.

"Come here."

Ginnie glared and backed up two steps.

"This way." He walked the opposite way toward the split-rail fence, leaned against it, and waited expectantly.

Ginnie imagined her feet turning into oak roots and scanned up and down the lane.

He cleared his throat and crooked his finger, his gaze never leaving her face. She thought back to the last time they went head to head like this. She swallowed. That didn't end well.

She took a step toward him and then stopped. *He's the one who's wrong. A mom? Where did that come from? I don't need a mom.*

His pointer finger went up.

Ginnie lifted her sneaker two inches and considered whether to stomp it or walk closer to him.

He arched an eyebrow and held up two fingers.

I hate it when he does that! Ginnie clenched her jaw, walked three steps toward him and stopped where the gravel met the grass. The grass sloped a little into a shallow ditch. The split rail fence was another four steps or so.

She glanced down the lane toward the farmhouse.

Nobody was walking around outside to help her and they wouldn't interfere anyway. Even Uncle Jake wouldn't get involved. Uncle Ben would tell her to "mind her dad" or "choose the right."

Dad wiggled the third finger, but didn't put it straight out.

Time's up. Once the finger straightens, I'm toast. Ginnie folded her arms, strode to the fence, and leaned against it, glaring across the lane.

"Well? I'm waiting."

And you're going to keep on waiting. Ginnie clamped her jaw shut tighter and turned away.

"Look at me."

She turned slightly in the opposite direction.

He blew out an impatient breath. "You heard me."

It took every bit of will power Ginnie had to ignore him.

"Fine." He walked around her and stopped when he stood directly in front of her.

She swallowed quickly and dropped her gaze to the gravel lane just beyond his boots.

"Really? That's the way you want to handle this?"

"Handle what?"

"This insanity that started out a civilized conversation ... before it took a sharp turn at crazy." He shook his head. "Tell me why you ran."

Ginnie shrugged and whirled from him.

"Turn around." When she ignored him, he walked around to face her again and lifted her chin firmly. "We've already played this game. I let you win ... *once*. Start acting like the twelve-year-old young woman you are or I'll treat you like the five-year-old brat you're behaving like."

She swallowed hard and searched his face. *Yikes, he's mad.*

"What happened?" He pointed down the lane to where she'd run from him, his voice softening. "You *agreed* that you and Tillie wanted Amanda and I to become better friends. I don't have a problem with that." He cleared his throat. "I mean, I understand why you'd want a mom. I missed my mom when she died. Beings how you're a girl, I know you need your mom even more than I needed mine."

Shaking her head, Ginnie silently cursed the burning behind her eyes. "You don't get it."

"Then talk to me until I do." His understanding tone took the wind out of her 'mad' sails.

Ginnie rolled her eyes and blinked several times, jutting her chin. "I just wanted Tillie and me to be sisters. That's it. I already told you. *I ... have ... Vi.*"

She could tell by the puzzled expression on his face he still didn't get it.

"How are you and Tillie supposed to be sisters if I don't marry Amanda? Not that I'm planning to or anything, but help me out here. People can only become sisters or brothers when their moms and dads get married. What am I missing?"

"Everything."

He took in a sharp breath and let it out slowly. "Being a smart aleck isn't helping."

She turned her face from his.

"Okay, so I'm supposed to adopt Tillie so you can have a sister and we're supposed to do *what* with Amanda? They're kind of a matched set. Like you, Toran, and I."

"You can marry her if you want." Ginnie threw her hands in the air. "I don't care. I already have a mom though ... and Vi. I *just* wanted a sister."

"Fair enough, you want a sister." He rubbed his thumb across her cheek, wiping a tear. "So what was Tillie's plan? Does she just want a sister? Because I'm not buying that."

"Why not?"

"Because ... and don't take this wrong." He winked at her. "Because even though you think I'm the 'Best Dad in the World' we both know I'm *not* perfect. Even so, Tillie's wanted me to be her dad since Jasper left."

Ginnie's mouth dropped open. "She's never said that."

Dad shrugged. "Maybe not in so many words, but her actions show it."

She thought about Tillie asking if Dad would adopt her and let her change her name to Tillie West. And how big she always smiled when Dad gave her attention.

It was Ginnie's turn to shake her head like an Etch-A-Sketch.

Tillie has turned "Operation: Secret Sisters" into "Operation: Steal My Dad!

34

BETRAYED

*D*ad leaned against the split-rail fence while Ginnie swiveled angrily in the grass in front of him.

"Tillie said that she wants *to ... be ... sisters.*" Ginnie practically spat the words.

"I'm sure she does, Gin." Dad hung his thumb on his front jean pocket. "She also wants a dad of her own. She was devastated when Jasper left, even though he hurt her."

Ginnie let his compassionate tone soothe the rising feelings of betrayal ... *a little.*

Dad drew her into his arms and tilted her chin up. "Don't be mad at her. Of course she wants a sister. And a dad. And a real family. You want your mama, don't you?"

Ginnie nodded.

"If I could, I would make our family whole again. But I can't. Tillie wants that too. It's the way things are supposed to be. Since her dad isn't here, Jake and I try to help her out now and again." He placed his hand on the post in front of them. "Remember when you were going to be my date for the go-karts and she was Jake's? And a couple weeks ago, Jake took you out for ice cream and I offered to take Tillie?"

She nodded again. Dad sighed and leaned against the fence. Ginnie thought about all the times she and Tillie 'double-dated' with Uncle Jake and Dad. "Yeah."

"When Grandma and Grandpa died, Uncle Ben and Aunt Sadie stepped in and did what they could to soften the blow of losing our folks. Jake and I try to do that for Tillie. And Vi and Amanda do that for *you*. Because as much as I'd like to be." He chuckled and held his fingers in the air for air quotes. "I know I'm not the 'best mom in the whole world'."

Ginnie giggled. "You're an okay mom *sometimes* though."

"I'm glad to hear that." He smiled and made a small arc in the grass with the heel of his cowboy boot. "I'm also hearing you did have a scheme about getting Amanda and me together, but I'm having a hard time believing you only thought you'd gain a sister. What role was Amanda supposed to play?"

Ginnie shrugged. "I didn't think about her being my stepmom. I guess I just thought Miss Amanda would still be Tillie's mom and somebody to make *you* happy."

He took a step back. "Well, that's a nice thought, but the only way I'd remarry is if I found a woman who wanted to be an awesome mom to my kids as well as a good friend to me. You and Toran are my life. I don't need anyone else in it to be happy."

"Even Uncle Jake?"

Dad chuckled. "He's my brother. For good or for bad, he'll always be around."

Ginnie scooted next to him. "I like that he's around."

"Yeah? Me too. *Most* of the time." Dad shook his head and smiled. "So, what's the next part of your scheme?"

Ginnie scrunched her face in thought. "I dunno. We only got as far as you and Miss Amanda wanting to date. But that part worked, didn't it?"

"Only because Amanda and I were friends already." He held his hand out. "After your mom died, I swore I would never date or remarry, at least until you and Toran were grown."

Ginnie let him hug her. "Why not?"

"Because good intentions aside, most people don't care about other people's kids as much as they do their own. I never want you and Toran to feel second rate—especially since you had the best mom in the whole world to start with." He wiggled his eyebrows playfully. "I picked her out special for you."

Laughing, Ginnie reached her arms around his waist. "You loved her that much?"

"I still do." He returned her hug.

"What about Miss Amanda? Do you love her?"

"I care about her. She's the only woman I've ever considered marrying since I lost your mom."

"Really?" Ginnie's mouth dropped open.

"You don't need to act so surprised. You and Tillie have talked about being sisters for years. Let's just say marrying Amanda has crossed my mind a time or two." He took in a breath and let it out slowly. "But it sounds like you'd rather have a sister than a mom."

"It's not that I don't want a mom. I *have* a mom." Ginnie jutted her chin, not quite making eye contact with him. "Or I would if *you'd* ever talk about her."

He stood straight, protesting. "I tell you about your mom."

Ginnie's hands perched on her hips. "No you don't. You always change the subject when she comes up. I haven't even seen a picture of her. She's like a big secret only *you* get to have."

Her angry tone startled Ginnie. The burning in her eyes returned, as did her urge to flee.

Dad's eyes widened. "That's not fair. I haven't changed the subject tonight and if you want to talk about her, then talk. I've been waiting for you to ask. Just ease up on the attitude."

"Waiting for me to ask? Since when?" Ginnie threw her hands in the air, frustration percolating like their old tea kettle. "How can I ask you about her? Whenever her name comes up, you look like you've lost your best friend."

"Because I *did* lose my best friend."

Ginnie had to let his words go through her mind twice before she heard them clearly. The sorrow in his voice forced tears to drown the burning she couldn't blink away. She glanced down the lane at the two-story farmhouse they called home, and fled toward it.

35

JUST A SWINGING...

ad's footsteps pounded the gravel behind her. She kept running. He didn't call out, but he did keep pace with her.

At the end of the lane, she scanned her options: the farmhouse ahead, the hay barn to the left, or the main barn up the hill. Before she could decide, Dad stood in front of her, blocking her way. "Come with me." He held out his hand.

Ginnie shoved her hands behind her back. She caught his eye briefly and looked away.

He took hold of her arm and slid his hand down to her wrist, then gripped her hand in his. With a gentle tug, Dad led them to the farmhouse.

Now I'm done for.

Uncle Ben sat on the porch swing, watching. When they reached the front porch, Dad stopped in front of the swing. "Sit with Uncle Ben."

After arching an eyebrow at Dad, Uncle Ben patted the seat next to him.

Ginnie glanced at Dad, debating whether she would obey.

He nodded at the swing.

Tired from her sprint, she dropped next to Uncle Ben, frustrated, and yet relieved.

Uncle Ben pumped the swing gently. Ginnie wiggled into the crook of his arm. The breeze felt cool on her face where tears had stained her cheeks. She wiped at them, trying to figure out what Dad would do when he came back.

A couple minutes later, he returned with a scrapbook and sat on Ginnie's other side. He adjusted the emerald green album on his lap.

Uncle Ben pointed at the book. "That's hers, isn't it?" His voice changed to a reverent whisper when he said "hers."

"Yes, sir." Dad sighed and looked at Ginnie. "I guess it's past time."

Uncle Ben stood. "I'll leave you two alone. If you need me, I'll be in the study."

Ginnie's heart pounded, first from concern that Uncle Ben was leaving, then excitement when she figured out who the "hers" was. She scooted closer to her dad.

He smiled and slid the book onto her lap. "I wanted to tell you that you were wrong about not seeing pictures of your mom, but the more I thought about it, the more I realized you were right. This starts when she's just a little older than you."

"For real?" Ginnie touched the cover, excitement pulsing through her like Christmas morning.

"For real."

She closed her eyes and concentrated on the face she could never quite recall. Imagining blue eyes and a pretty smile, she still couldn't see Mama's nose or eyebrows clearly. She remembered a floral perfume and Mama's long curly blonde hair tickling her cheeks when Mama reached for her to help her off her horse, Eternal Love. Ginnie glanced at Dad.

"Go ahead and open it." He didn't need to tell her twice.

She lifted the cover and blinked to make sure she wasn't dreaming. Letting the cover rest on Dad's lap, she sucked in a sharp breath. There, in front of her very eyes, was the mother she'd been trying to remember.

And Mama didn't look like a mom at all.

She looks ... like ... ME.

36

THE SCRAPBOOK

$\mathcal{G}$innie darted a quick glance to Dad and then back to the page in front of her. The caption read: Ginnie (14).

"That's *my* name."

"Yes." Dad pumped the swing. "That's probably weird for you. I only knew her as 'Ginnie' the first couple times I met her. When she told me about all the titles she won as a rodeo and beauty queen, I started calling her 'Queenie.' Then I fell in love with her and she became 'The queen of my heart.'"

"Geez, Dad, I knew I was a junior, but really ... I'm a clone." She elbowed him lightly, teasing. "I didn't even get my own nickname. And I look *just* like her. Without makeup."

"You're technically a 'second' and it wasn't *her* nickname anymore. She's 'Queenie' to me. Ginnie is *you*. And what did you want us to call you, 'Virgie'?"

"Virgie?" Ginnie mimed sticking her finger down her throat. "I guess 'Ginnie' works."

He chuckled. "That's what I thought, but she used to call you Tallulah."

"Yuck—I'm not sure what's worse, Virgie or Tallulah? They're both gross."

"Which is why we went with Ginnie." He touched the photo and smiled. "But personally, I liked Tallulah."

"Seriously?"

"Yes. One day, the three of you blinged out three pairs of sunglasses with jewels. I came home from work and you were decked out as 'Tallulah Hollywood', complete with an emerald green feather boa. She called Toran: 'Sergio Screenplay' and gave him a silky yellow handkerchief for his pocket. You guys even put on a play for me."

"Really? Did you record it?"

"I did. It will take some digging, but I'll find it for you." He sighed softly. "Your mom was in it. It would be fun for you and your brother to watch."

Ginnie traced the picture of Mama with her eyes. She wore a pink cowboy hat with a white feather hat band. Her blonde hair bounced in curls around her shoulders. The pink buttoned down shirt matched the hat and was opened to show a white shirt. Her dazzling smile jumped off the page. "She's beautiful."

"She is. When you were born, I was glad you looked like her." He laughed and tapped the page. "Now that I see boys looking at you, I wish you didn't look *so* much like her."

Ginnie's cheeks heated. "Boys don't look at me."

"Hah!" Dad tapped the page harder. "You just don't pay attention. But *I* do. And I will *keep* paying attention."

"That sounds like a threat."

"*You* can consider it a warning." He laughed again and turned the page. "Boys who think they want to date you, *they* can consider it a threat."

Ginnie shook her head and grimaced. "Vi's right. You *are* a Neanderthal."

"I'm also your dad. Nobody dates you without going through me. But you wanted to talk about your mom, so let's talk. We can discuss dating when you're thirty-seven."

After rolling her eyes, she focused on the head shot of her mom. "How old was she here? She looks a lot older." Ginnie scanned the page for the date of the photo. "Hey, according to this, she's only a month older."

"Make-up will do that. This photo was part of her portfolio--what they judged her facial beauty on." He pumped the swing a little. "Just so you know I am very okay with you being a tomboy and *not* wanting to wear make-up. It's one thing to see my wife like this, but I'm not looking forward to the day our daughter follows in her footsteps. I'm thinking no make-up until you're twenty-three works for me. What do *you* think?" His nervous laugh made her giggle.

"I don't care right now, but if I change my mind it should be worth something."

"You certainly are your mother's daughter. Just forget I said anything."

"Too late." She considered making a joke, but decided he'd retaliate by raising her dating age to forty-seven, so Ginnie giggled softly and peeked at the next photo of Mama.

Mama's hair was swept into an updo with a few blonde wispy curls framing her face. The facing page had a full body pose of her in a sparkling sapphire blue-and-silver dress, draped with three sashes that read: Prettiest Eyes, Best Overall Facial Beauty, and Ultimate Queen Supreme with a trophy at her feet that towered above the one foot high diamond tiara crown on her head. There were four smaller trophies at her feet as well.

Dad pointed at the trophies. "This was a full glitz pageant. See the sequins and jewels all over her dress? She's beautiful, but I prefer the rodeo pictures that show her natural beauty."

He flipped the page and let Ginnie peek at four more pages of pageantry photos, each with her mom looking perfect and older, dressed in breathtaking gowns and different hairstyles. In every picture Mama wore several sashes and held various prizes, from giant teddy bears, to a new DVD player to a fan made out of twenty dollar bills.

Each photo contained at least three trophies and two crowns, which were really tiaras of different heights and shapes. "How did she always win so many crowns at one competition?"

"She placed well in her age division and then in overall categories because she scored so high. She cleaned up at most pageants. But look." He turned the page. "This is what I wanted you to see. Here she is in her riding competitions."

Mama either sat astride or stood next to a beautiful Thoroughbred horse much like Calliope in several of the next photos. She wore cowboy hats in different colors, some with sequins and jewels and a couple with tiaras as hat bands.

In all of them, Ginnie could see the pure joy that riding held for her mom.

"That's Eternal Love, right?" Ginnie pointed to her mom's mount.

"Yes. Love was born on her twelfth birthday. They've been together ever since."

"Where's she now?"

"I don't know. Martin didn't have her anymore when he offered you Calliope."

"Why'd you sell her? She was special to Mama." Ginnie frowned and glanced from Dad to Eternal Love, scolding. "You should have kept her."

"And do *what* with her? She mourned for Queenie too. Your mom was the horse whisperer, not me. I was in no condition to be a therapist for a horse. It was hard enough keeping myself sane."

Ginnie searched Dad's face. "Love mourned for Mama?"

"Yes." Dad leaned back in the swing. "It was heartbreaking to see her listless and off her feed. She was never the same after the accident."

"But she liked *me*. I bet I could've made her feel better."

"No way was I letting you near that horse after the accident." He lifted her chin and looked her in the eye. "Keeping my sanity, and you and Toran safe, was all I could manage."

Ginnie swallowed hard. After she turned the page, Dad let his gaze rest on a picture of Mama holding a trophy in one hand, her other arm slid under Eternal Love's neck in a hug, her smile even more dazzling. "Martin was kind to Love. He wanted her even before the accident. So when I sold her to him, he bred her with his best sire and she had Calliope."

He pulled his wallet out and opened it to a picture of young Ginnie sitting on a horse.

"That's me on Eternal Love."

He nodded. "You were three-and-a-half. Your mom took it about a month before she died." He pointed at Mama's smile and then the big grin on young Ginnie's face.

"Notice anything?" He flapped the smaller photo. "This picture is what made me change my mind about keeping Calliope."

Ginnie snapped her face toward his. "Really?"

He nodded. "Look at your smiles. Whenever she rode, her smile was even more dazzling, brighter. Like a flashlight with new batteries. Riding with her did the same thing for you." His eyes searched her face. "I want you to have that charge. I just don't want you to do tricks. I won't take a chance on losing you as well."

"When Mr. Davis saw us at the rodeo and offered Calliope to me I was so excited." Ginnie rubbed her palms on her jeans. "Then you said 'no'. I didn't understand why at first."

"I know you didn't. And then you cried until you threw up, begging and pleading, until I thought I'd lose my mind." He tapped the picture again. "Do you remember that?"

"Yeah. But you didn't seem to care."

He sighed. "I cared, but I was afraid of losing you. Then Uncle Ben suggested you could have Calliope, but not as a trick horse. I wanted to see this smile again." Dad lifted her chin. "Martin was dying of cancer and wanted you to have Calliope. He told me that Queenie's daughter and Eternal Love's daughter belonged together. He was right."

Ginnie tried to mimic the smile in the picture. "You know that morning you told me we were keeping Calliope? I realized you said no because you didn't want me to get hurt like Mama did. And that you weren't just being mean."

"You thought I was being mean?"

Ginnie shrugged. "I didn't know why you wouldn't want me to

have my own horse, especially since her mom was *my* mom's horse. I realized you were scared I'd get hurt so I decided to quit nagging you." Ginnie grinned bigger. "But you told me I could have her before I could get the words out."

Dad winked. "Maybe I should have held out a little longer."

"No way! I kept my word. I don't do tricks on her, but I could barrel race like Mama." She pointed at the money fan. "I could do that. It's just riding in circles fast. I wouldn't get hurt."

"No way. If I let you barrel race, you'll want to do other competitions and you'll try crazy things. Your mom did. But you don't have the training she did." Dad shook his head. "And she's not here to help you."

"But I won't be crazy. I promise."

"I said *no!*" His sharp tone made her glue her eyes to his. "You should know I have people wanting to buy Calliope. I could sell her and make enough money to fund your first year of college." He pointed his finger at her. "The only reason I *don't* is because you love her so much. But if you go behind my back and do tricks on her, you can consider her sold."

She reeled backward. "You wouldn't."

Flying over the hood of Mrs. MacGregor's car flashed through her mind. The feeling of being free and part of Calliope beckoned her.

"I would." He closed the wallet and softened his tone. "I'd hate it, but I would. Don't put me in a position where I have to."

She sat straight up. "But she's *my* horse. You can't sell *my* horse."

"I certainly can. *My* name's on her pedigree." He leaned against the back of the swing. "And I will ... if you break your word. There's no compromise here, Gin. There will be no tricks and no competitions ... unless you want there to be no Calliope."

His words bounced a torrent of emotions inside her.

She looked to Mama, but her smile didn't help the gloomy feelings storming inside. *No Calliope?*

37

NO CALLIOPE?

*H*eart pounding, Ginnie fisted her hands, trying to get a grip. Wild thoughts of screaming her outrage, throwing the album, and bolting down the lane crashed against one another as she tried to breathe through her dad's threat.

"Ginnie, you can keep Calliope." Dad's quiet voice broke into her tumbling thoughts. "Our agreement has worked for three years. There's no reason anything has to change. This isn't new information, other than people are interested in buying Calliope."

"Who wants her?" Ginnie pounded the swing seat with her fist, hissing. "She's mine!"

"Calm down."

She glared at him, too many thoughts zipping around her head to express one calmly.

He rested a hand on her fisted one.

She snatched it away and scooted to the front of the swing, stopping just before she jumped off when Dad shook his head.

He cleared his throat. "You're just hearing you'll lose Calliope. That's *not* what I said. I've had some generous offers to buy her, but I've never considered them for more than a minute."

"Why not?" Her voice dripped with suspicion.

"Because you love Calliope." He turned toward her. "You shouldn't be surprised that she's valuable for breeding. She's a pure-bred and her mother was a one-of-a-kind grand champion." He winked at her. "Just like *your* mother. Er, her being one-of-a-kind—that is. She was a grand champion in everything she did too. She made the best kids in the whole world. And she was the best friend I could ever ask for."

"That's not funny." Ginnie shook her head. "Why would you threaten to sell Calliope?"

"It's not a threat. It's a promise." Dad sighed and rubbed a hand on his jeans. "And it's not something I'm going to argue with you about." He turned on his 'lecture' voice. "As long as you leave things alone, you have nothing to worry about. If you change the terms of our agreement without permission, I'll make some phone calls and Calliope will find a new home. It's entirely up to you."

She fisted her hands and then unclenched them. *But I want things to change. I want you to let me be who I need to be.* Ginnie swallowed her protests. "Would you let me if Mama were here?"

He chuckled. "I wouldn't have a choice. Your mom had you in a baby sling riding the second day you were home from the hospital. She had all sorts of plans for you and Toran to follow in her footsteps. She even planned to buy each of you a pony for your fourth birthday."

Ginnie's eyes popped. "That didn't happen, did it?"

He shook his head. "No. After I sold Eternal Love, I decided never to own another horse."

"I'm glad Uncle Ben helped you change your mind." She offered an impish grin. "What did Uncle Jake say about it?"

"What do *you* think he said?"

"That you were being an overprotective stick-in-the-mud."

He nodded and then laughed. "That pretty much sums it up." Dad patted the swing seat and waited for her to scoot back. "You know Gin, as much as I'd like to be your friend, I need to be your dad first. Sometimes that means telling you 'no' and letting you be angry."

She offered him her best smile. "Or you could compromise and say I could barrel race, but not do tricks, and we can both be happy and miserable—but more *happy* than miserable."

He grinned. "True. Or you could just quit bugging me while you still have a horse."

Ginnie's smile dimmed. "Do you think you'll ever change your mind?"

"Talk to me when pigs fly." He turned a page. "Do you want to finish looking at this, or do something else?"

"Keep telling me about my mom."

"I can do that."

38

SORTING THINGS OUT

Tillie hugged her knees to her chest and rocked on her bed, concentrating on the friendly wink DT offered her when he closed the door to Mom's car just before they left the farm.

She pushed away the nagging feeling that Ginnie was no longer on board with OSS. Sure, Ginnie seemed angry during church, weird during Sunday school, but by the time everybody got to the farm, she was her normal friendly self.

Maybe tomorrow she'll let me know why she was so weird.

Mom knocked on her door.

"Come in."

Mom entered with a big smile on her face, but it faded when she saw Tillie. "Is something wrong, honey?"

Sliding her legs down the magenta comforter, Tillie smiled. "I'm fine, just thinking. You look happy."

"I am. It was fun playing 'tag' at the farm today. It's been a long time since I ran like that."

"That *was* fun. Uncle Jake is really fast—and sneaky."

"But not as fast as Todd. It was fun watching those two act like kids. I always wanted a big brother."

Tillie giggled. "I'm sure he'll give you Uncle Jake." *Of course if you marry DT, Uncle Jake becomes your big brother automatically.*

"Todd was telling me how Jake used to pick on him as a kid. Jake was a bit of a bully."

"No way. Not Uncle Jake. He's a tease, but he's nice." Tillie pushed her bangs out of her eyes.

"Grief will make you do some crazy things. Todd let a lot of things slide because he wanted Jake to like him and they were all that was left of their original family."

"That's like you. Only you don't have a brother."

Mom sighed. "My sister and I will never be close. She's too much like our dad—mean and selfish. I don't blame her for the way she turned out, but I don't want that drama in your life. Once I got away from it, I swore I'd never go back. Then I met Jasper." Mom locked her eyes on Tillie's. "Promise me you'll listen to me if I ever tell you that you're dating somebody like him. I don't want you to make the same mistake I did."

Tillie reeled backward on her bed. "I would *never* date someone like him. He's awful."

"He wasn't when I met him. When he focused on us, he could be very thoughtful. But then he'd get frustrated or discouraged and forget what was important and become that scared kid he used to hate being." Mom sat on the bed beside her and smiled. "But he did give me the best kid in the whole world."

Tillie leaned on her elbow. "Well, that's true, but still ... I could never date someone like him."

"What kind of someone *could* you date?"

Tapping her finger on her cheek, she smiled at Mom. "Someone like Ginnie's dad. He's nice and he doesn't yell."

Oops, I don't want Mom to think I'm setting her up, she might not cooperate. She added in a hurry. "Though Uncle Jake is a lot of fun. Or even Buzz; he's quiet and really seems to like Faith. He actually blushed when Ginnie and I caught them kissing on the front porch."

"Kissing, huh? Then he must be getting serious." Mom's eyes

shone as she giggled. "I wonder what Uncle Ben thinks. Maybe he'll have two weddings soon."

"Two?" Tillie sat straight up. *You and DT?*

Her heart pounded in her ears.

"Now that Vi's engagement is official, there will be all kinds of wedding plans to make. Vi, Lauren, and I have already planned to shop for flowers, her cake, and all."

Duh. Preston just proposed. "Yeah, that was a pretty cool way to propose." Tillie pasted a smile on her lips to hide her disappointment. "And Uncle Ben didn't give Preston any trouble about saying 'yes'. Well, not much anyway."

Mom giggled. "As nice as the West men are, they can be intimidating when it comes to someone wanting to date, let alone marry, one of their women. Todd is already practicing the interview process that anyone wanting to date you and Ginnie will be going through."

"Me?" Tillie's heart pounded quicker.

"Of course. He's very protective of you. So's Jake. And Uncle Ben. And Buzz." Mom shook her head, laughing. "They may be Neanderthals, but they're *sweet* Neanderthals. I like that they care."

"Me too." Tillie let Mom's words glide over her like glaze on a fresh donut. *Even if OSS doesn't work out, DT still cares about me. That's cool.*

"Vi finds them annoying, but she doesn't know what it's like to have a dad who doesn't care." Mom's voice caught. She stared at Tillie, and then patted her leg. "Your dad cares about you. That's why he left. So he wouldn't hurt us anymore. He wanted better for you than he had."

Tillie jumped to her feet. "Then he should have stopped drinking. He knows that alcohol makes him mean. If he *really* cared about me, he would have changed."

"Tils, he cares. He was sick. And his parents were super awful, worse than mine." Mom stood and brushed Tillie's hair from her eyes. "Don't hate him. One day you might see him again and realize he isn't all bad."

Tillie froze. *See him again?*

"No way! I never want to see him again, ever."

"He's your father. He has rights, Tillie."

"Not anymore. He left."

Mom shook her head, pressing her lips tightly together.

"Right? He can't just show up here ... can he?" Tillie locked her eyes on Mom's. *I picked a new dad. You're in love with DT ... Jasper's history.*

"Jasper isn't part of our family anymore. He doesn't get to be here, right?"

Mom sighed. "I wish that were true."

Tillie's belly heaved. She gulped, trying to fight the overwhelming nausea. She shook her head, pleading. "He *can't* come back."

"I can't promise you he won't come back."

"*But he'll ruin everything.*"

"Not if he's changed."

Tillie's hands flew to her hips. "How would you know if he's changed? It's not like you talk to him." Her eyes narrowed in suspicion. "You *don't* talk to him, do you?"

Mom took a step backward. "He writes or calls every once in a while."

"And you didn't tell me?" Tillie glared until Mom lowered her gaze.

"Because it upsets you. He does love you, Tillie." Mom offered a half-hearted laugh and tried to hug her. "What's not to love? You're a great kid. Of course he wants to be part of your life."

Tillie pushed Mom's arm away, not wanting a hug. "You're not going to let him, are you?"

Mom turned away.

"You're not letting him come back ... *are you?*" Panic surged with the rise of each syllable.

"To live with us, no. But if he's changed, he can get a lawyer and maybe see you."

Tillie's heart pounded as her throat went dry. "I don't want to see him."

Mom slipped an arm around her shoulders. "It's not something we have to worry about tonight."

"When *do* we need to worry about it?"

Mom shrugged and held her tight, her silence pounding louder than Tillie's heart.

39

QUEEN OF DAD'S HEART

*A*s the pages turned, Mama grew from a fourteen-year-old girl to a nineteen-year-old woman.

Ginnie listened while Dad talked about Mama. The stories got more detailed toward the end of the book.

"After she brushed me off the second time, I bought her a brush that I decorated with rhinestones that said: 'Queen of my Heart.' She actually laughed and told me I had ten minutes to explain why she should even give me *those* ten minutes."

"Did that make you mad?"

He chuckled. "Nope. I finally had her undivided attention."

"What did you tell her?"

"That I only needed *two* minutes. I told her I loved her and if she'd take a chance on me I'd make sure she'd never regret it. I knew without a doubt we would be together forever."

"And she believed you?"

"Not at first." He shook his head. "But I held her hands, looked into her eyes, and asked her to pray about it, because I already had, and I knew we were supposed to be together."

"What did she say?"

"She laughed."

"Ouch." Ginnie giggled.

"I'll say." He chuckled again, shaking his head. "I just repeated that I knew we were meant to be together and that my life wouldn't be complete without her, and hers wouldn't be complete without me. She stopped laughing and asked, 'You're really serious, aren't you?'"

"Wow, Daddy. I just can't see you taking a chance like that."

"When I look back, I can't believe it either. I'd never even taken chances on quiet girls, and she was a hurricane. I was completely out of my league. I needed her just as much as I needed oxygen to breathe." His eyes brightened as he spoke. "There was just something about her. Intoxicating—in a good way, of course. Courting her was a wild ride."

"So it was love at first sight?"

"For me." Dad released a slow breath. "On the other hand, being drop-dead gorgeous and a beauty queen, she had a lot of suitors and didn't see why she should give me the time of day. I offered her my heart and my love. I guess that was enough, because she said 'yes.'"

Ginnie beamed. "I'm glad she said 'yes.'"

Dad hugged her tight. "Me too."

The second to the last page had an envelope tucked into it. Ginnie opened the envelope and found several more pictures of her mother as a young child and at twenty, with two babies in her arms and Dad with his arms around the three of them.

"Wow!" Ginnie waved the picture in his face. "That's us! That's our whole family!"

"Yes, Queenie insisted on the coordinated rodeo outfits." He took the photo out of her hand and held it where they could both see it.

Dad and Toran wore matching sapphire blue satin rodeo shirts. Ginnie wore a hot pink rodeo shirt and skirt while Mama's was emerald green. All four of them smiled brightly. Mama looked so happy. Ginnie had on hot pink cowboy boots, while Toran wore sapphire blue.

"Your mama special ordered those boots. She even cried when you guys outgrew them."

"Did you save them?"

"She did. I'm not sure where they are."

"Look how adorable she was in this picture!" Ginnie squealed, holding a picture of three-year-old Ginnie West as Little Miss Sweet Potato.

Dad laughed. "That's not her, that's *you*."

"No way! I was never in a pageant."

"Yes way, you certainly were. Look." Dad pointed at her name. "Her picture would say Ginnie Stratton, not Ginnie West. She didn't go by Queenie until just before she married me." He laughed at some memory, and then stopped talking.

"Please keep telling me about Mama."

Dad sighed. "I told you she had a great imagination, right?"

"Yeah."

"Well, she would make up these fairytale stories about our life, complete with castles, dragons, and our prince and princess that sounded so real. I let myself be whisked away in the fantasy of it all. We had an incredible life. Like magic, only better, because it was real." He paused like he was deciding whether or not to tell her anymore.

Ginnie held her breath, hoping he would keep sharing.

"When she died, my Queen was gone." His voice cracked. He shifted against the back of the swing. "Reality hit and it hit hard. The three of us moved in here. You two started preschool. The fairytale world I shared with your mama disappeared."

"That's sad," Ginnie whispered.

"It is." He blew out a quiet breath. "Anyway, you were in several pageants. Toran too."

Ginnie shook her head, scanning her memory. "You're kidding, right?"

"No. You both won first place in the Prince and Princess Sugar Plum pageant when you were seven months old, your first Christmas."

"Why didn't you ever tell me before?"

Dad shrugged. "Pageants were your mama's thing. They were part of the fairytale life. I'd never really cared for them and when she died, so did my interest in them. Besides, I'm not sure I would've let you keep competing in them as you got older anyway, even if she'd lived."

"Would Mama have let us?"

"Not if I didn't agree. Toran didn't like them as much as you did. But he liked being Sergio to your Tallulah." Dad laughed and mimed holding a microphone. "You two rocked at your final Thanksgiving pageant. You won 'Ultimate Queen Supreme'. And five hundred dollars."

"Five hundred bucks?" Ginnie's eyes popped.

"Yes. It's in your college fund, so no, you can't spend it."

"Five hundred dollars for smiling and dressing up?"

"Yes, but we spent more than that on your dress and entry fees. You won a thousand at a different pageant. It's a very expensive hobby, but with your mom as your coach, it was more of an investment. You always placed high."

"A thousand bucks? No way."

"Yes way." He pointed to a photo of Mama as the 'Grand Supreme Queen'. "Even though these are gorgeous pictures of your mom, my favorites are the ones where she's holding or playing with you and Toran. She loved you two so much. I see that love in her eyes every time I see a picture of her looking at either of you."

His words poured over her like warm syrup on a stack of homemade pancakes.

"You did pick us the best mom in the whole world, huh?"

"I absolutely did."

On the last page was a picture of Mama in her final rodeo competition. She wore the same outfit as in their family photo and stood next to Eternal Love. She smiled, holding a huge Grand Championship trophy. Dad stood next to her, with Ginnie in one arm and Toran in the other.

"We looked like the perfect fairytale family," Ginnie gushed.

"We *were* the perfect fairytale family," Dad whispered.

Ginnie twisted to look at him. A tear rolled down his cheek. "You really miss her, don't you?"

"I do." He wiped away the tear.

"I'm sorry."

"For what?"

"Just because." Ginnie snuggled against his chest. She felt the tingle of a few tear drops on top of her head.

He hugged her tight. Tears continued to drop on the crown of her head. "I'm sorry, Gin."

"It's okay. I miss her too."

He wiped his eyes with the sleeve of his t-shirt. "You probably don't remember this, but after your mom died, I was so lost. It was even worse than when my folks died. I felt so alone and overwhelmed. It hurt even to breathe."

At least a minute passed before he spoke again. He wound one of her braids around his finger. "One day, Maybe a week after her funeral, I was sitting on the couch and you came over and asked what was wrong. Since you were just three-and-a-half, I told you I was fine."

Dad offered a soft chuckle. "But you saw straight through me. You wagged your finger and told me 'that I was not either fine' and stomped your foot at me. You crawled into my lap and said you were going to help me cry, because then I'd feel better."

Ginnie smiled, picturing herself as he described. "Did you cry?"

"Not at first. But you wrapped your arms around my neck and laid your head on my shoulder and told me to take my time." He exhaled. "Of course, I was determined not to, but you stayed quiet, so unlike your normal busy self. Then you said you'd cry with me, because you missed her so much too. After you started crying, I couldn't help but join you."

He shifted so he could see her. "You were right. I did feel better. Thanks for that."

"Anytime." She snuggled into his arms, the rhythm of his heart beating like a lullaby.

40

TWINKLE TOES, SNUGG'EMS, PUMPKIN, OR SUGAR PIE?

*D*ad? Hey, Dad!" Toran's footsteps pounded down the stairs. "Where are you?"

Ginnie jerked upright.

"On the porch, Tor." Dad wiped his cheeks and motioned for Toran to join them.

Her twin opened the screen door.

Ginnie swiped at her eyes and smiled. "Hey, check this out. Daddy's showing me Mama's competition scrapbook."

Toran did a double-take. "*Our* mom's scrapbook? With *pictures*?"

"Okay, okay. So maybe I haven't been as open about her as I thought I'd been. Sit down and I'll make it up to you." Dad stopped the swing, had Ginnie move over a little, and patted the empty spot next to him. "Wait. Did you need me for something?"

"I wanted to show you this cool photo program I've been playing with, but seeing pictures of Mama is better. Why didn't you come get me so I could see them too?"

"Sorry. I was trying to fix something between Ginnie and me, and I should have included you as well." Dad patted the swing again. "Have a seat and we'll catch you up."

Toran sat. Dad opened the scrapbook.

"When did you have a pink cowboy hat, Ginnie? And why are you in Mama's scrapbook? Is there a picture of me?" Toran looked from Dad to Ginnie.

Ginnie laughed.

"That's not your sister, that's your mother." Dad pointed to her name. "Ginnie is what your mama went by before I married her." He went on to explain how they met and gave a quick overview of several of the stories he had shared with Ginnie.

Ginnie opened the envelope and showed Toran their family picture in rodeo clothes.

"Geez, Dad, are those clothes bright enough? Where'd you find the matching hats and boots?"

Dad shrugged. "I dunno. Your mom found all kinds of interesting get-ups. I just went along with her. I wanted a family portrait. She wanted us to coordinate. We got along so well because she cared about the details and I didn't." He tapped the photo. "My job was to show up, help her dress you guys, and get you to smile. I did my job, and this picture looks pretty good."

"I think we're adorable," Ginnie said.

"Well, yeah, we're cute, but you kinda need shades to look at this picture." Toran squinted and held it closer. "Do you have any more photos of us as a family?"

Dad flipped to the last page of the scrapbook. "Just this one at the moment."

"Speaking of shades, do you have any pictures of us as Sergio and Tallulah?"

"As who?" Toran asked.

Ginnie laughed at his puzzled expression. "Mama called you Sergio Screenplay and me Tallulah Hollywood."

Toran's mouth formed a capital 'O.' "And why would she do that?"

"Because she liked nicknames and make-believe." Dad pointed to Mama in the last photo. "Your mom was a lot of fun."

Ginnie smiled. "What nickname did she give *you*?"

Dad's cheeks pinked. He looked at his watch. "It's bedtime."

"No fair changing the subject. What did she call you?" Toran insisted.

"A lot of things. It depended on her mood. I liked 'honey' and 'my hero' the best." He shut the scrapbook and stood. "And it's still bedtime."

"Those are pretty lame compared to Tallulah and Sergio." Ginnie stood next to him. "What did she call you for reals?"

"She didn't like spiders." The screen door squeaked as he opened it, joining his protest. "So I squished them for her and I was her hero. It worked for us."

"Todd the Terminator." Toran quipped, tapping Ginnie's elbow and laughing. "I'll bet it was something embarrassing like Hunky Monkey, or Twinkle Toes, or Fabulous Fabio."

"Or maybe: 'Nunya' as in: none of your business." Dad waved them into the house. "G'nite."

"That's s-o-o-o not fair." Ginnie walked inside. "You said you'd share her with us."

"What's not fair?" Uncle Jake asked, coming down the stairs with Vi.

"I did share her with you." Dad pointed up the stairs. "Go brush your teeth."

Uncle Jake and Vi moved over to the entryway. Ginnie reached the first step. "Uncle Jake, Daddy won't tell us what Mama used to call him."

Uncle Jake winked. "Oh, you mean like Hunka Hunka Burnin' Love? Or Hot Stuff or ..."

Dad took a step toward his brother. "Or 'You can stop talking now'."

"That could be, but I don't remember that one." Uncle Jake ducked when Dad raised his fist.

Ginnie, Toran, and Vi burst out laughing.

"Not funny, Jacob Douglas."

Uncle Jake hitched his thumb at Ginnie and Toran. "They think it is."

"You've made him mad now, the dreaded middle name," Vi

teased. "I liked it when she called him Snugg'ems or Sugar Pie. There was just something about her southern accent. I liked the way she said 'pie.' Sugar pie ... honey pie ... sweetie pie."

Toran doubled over laughing.

Dad folded his arms across his chest. "Violet Elizabeth, you'd better stop."

Vi wagged a scolding finger. "Why Todd Benjamin, you're *not* my dad."

The study door opened. All heads turned toward Uncle Ben. "But *I* am and you *do* need to stop." Uncle Ben sent Vi and Uncle Jake warning looks.

"There's another blast from the past." Uncle Jake nodded at Dad. "You taking *his* side."

Uncle Ben strode over to the screen door and opened it. "You're welcome to take a walk with me and discuss it."

"Yah? I don't think so." Uncle Jake backed up a step. "But thanks for the offer."

Ginnie giggled.

"What're you afraid of?" Dad squared himself to Uncle Jake. "You're bigger than he is."

"Like that matters. You and me." Uncle Jake wiggled his finger from Dad to himself. "We'll finish this later. Him and me?" Uncle Jake winked at Ginnie. "I'll pass on."

Uncle Ben chuckled. "It's good to know I raised you right."

Uncle Jake shook his head and opened his eyes wide in mock terror. "Raised, intimidated, scared the tar out of, whatever you want to call it ... it's all good."

Ginnie smiled. "Uncle Ben's not scary. He's a teddy bear."

"Whatever helps you sleep at night. Speaking of which ..." Uncle Jake motioned at the stairs and winked. "Pleasant dreams. Sugarlips will be along shortly to tuck you in."

"You are s-o-o on," Dad threatened.

Uncle Ben cleared his throat. "You two can take it outside with me after these two go to bed."

Uncle Jake rolled his eyes. "Thanks a lot, Sugarlips."

"You're welcome, *Not*-So-Hot-Stuff." Dad grimaced at Uncle Jake and then pointed up the staircase for Ginnie and Toran's benefit. "Good night."

"Night," they chorused. Ginnie's hand flew to her mouth to stifle a giggle as she hurried up the stairs.

41

HUNKA HUNKA DADDY?

Ginnie turned over in her bed, restless, and kicked back the covers. Dad sure was taking a long time saying good night to Toran. All the things he told her tonight ran through her mind.

How she used to be in pageants, how he had people wanting to buy Calliope, how much Mama really loved Toran and her, and how much Daddy really loved her mom.

How he had sort of known about OSS, even though he got it all wrong. Ginnie sat up in a panic.

OSS!

What am I going to tell Tillie?

After jerking her emerald green comforter around her chin, she punched her pillow. She adjusted a second pillow and then scrunched her favorite one and lay back down.

"Are you mad? Or just can't get comfortable?" Dad asked, entering her room.

Ginnie shrugged. "I'm hot and not tired. And I don't know what to tell Tillie."

"Tell Tillie about what?"

"OSS."

"OSS?"

"Nothing." Ginnie turned away from him.

"What's OSS?"

"Just something we made up. But you kinda ruined it."

"Is OSS your scheme to get Amanda and me together?"

"Yeah, but not quite. It stands for Operation: Secret Sisters, but now it's probably Operation: Not Gonna Happen."

"Why not?' Dad pointed to her bed. "May I?"

Ginnie sighed and then nodded. "You loved Mama. You aren't going to marry Miss Amanda."

Dad sat next to her. "While it's true that I loved your mama very much and I still do, I like the idea of spending more time with Amanda. It feels nice to have someone to share things with, especially with someone who already loves my kids."

Ginnie grinned. "You mean you want to marry her?"

His hands flew up in a 'whoa' motion. "I didn't say that. I mean I want to think about dating her and see how it goes. And I want you and Toran to be okay with it. But you talked a lot about wanting Tillie for a sister and wanting to get to know your mom. I want to be fair to you *and* Amanda. If you can't find it in you to want a new mom, then I'm not going to pursue this right now. The three of us are doing fine and we'll keep doing fine."

Falling back on her pillows, Ginnie considered his words. After a minute, she leaned on her elbow. "If I had to pick a mom besides mine, it would be Miss Amanda. She does love us and treats us good. If you want to date her, you should."

Dad brushed a strand of hair out of her face. "I never thought I'd be asking my daughter's permission to date, but I'll admit I feel better knowing you're okay with this."

"Tillie wants to know if you'll let her change her last name to West. Will you?'

Dad chuckled. "She's given this a bit of thought, huh?"

"It was kind of *her* idea." Ginnie shrugged.

"Well, I don't have a problem with that. But you're both forgetting about Amanda. We've only been on one date. She might decide she doesn't like me after all."

"Nope." Ginnie shook her head, recalling the looks passing between Miss Amanda and Dad all afternoon. "She's crushing on you."

He smiled. "How do you know?"

She rolled her eyes. "Because I'm a woman. We know these things."

"Stop that." Dad tweaked her nose. "Woman or not, that bugs me." He smiled and stood. "I'll call Amanda tomorrow and see if she's busy. I work days, so tomorrow night's free. Unless you and Tillie have made some other plans I should know about?"

Ginnie shook her head and laughed.

He leaned down and kissed her forehead. "Goodnight, Tallulah Hollywood."

"Night, Daddy."

He strode across the room. As he reached for the light switch, Ginnie asked, giggling. "So ... did Mama *really* call you Hunka Hunka Burnin' Love?"

Dad's mouth dropped open and he muttered something under his breath. The only thing Ginnie made out was Uncle Jake's name and a frustrated tone.

"I called her Queenie, she liked Elvis, and he was 'the king'." He turned a little too quickly and snapped off the light. "It worked for us. Good night."

He closed the door and left before Ginnie could say another word. *That wasn't a 'no'.*

She giggled again and lay back on her pillows, pretty sure Uncle Jake was in big trouble.

42

OSS IS OVER

*W*hen a shadow crossed Ginnie in the hen house, she looked up expectantly, smiling at Tillie.

Tillie smiled back. "Hi, Gin."

"Hey. Come in, I've got stuff to tell you."

"You sound happy. What's up?" Tillie opened the bottom half of the door.

"Daddy knows about OSS."

Tillie froze in the doorway.

"It's okay. He wants to date your mom."

Tillie flapped her hands and squealed. "He said that?"

Ginnie nodded and plucked a piece of straw off an egg. "Yep. And guess what?"

"What?"

"He actually showed me a scrapbook of my mom. She looks like me—or me like her. No wonder he looks at me like he sees a ghost sometimes. I thought he just missed her a lot, but I really look like her, except she's gorgeous."

Tillie frowned. "You're gorgeous too. I tell you all the time you waste being a girl."

"No, Tillie. She's like super ultimate gorgeous. Like remember I told you she was a beauty queen? She won thousands of dollars and teddy bears and TVs and all kinds of stuff. Oh, and get this, I used to be in pageants too."

"No way!"

"Yes, and I won money too. Daddy says it was because Mama was my coach, but I didn't remember—though last night I had a dream about being in a pageant. Mama was clapping for me. Until last night, I only remembered riding Eternal Love with her."

"Wow! That must make you happy."

Ginnie shrugged and put an egg in the basket. "It does, but it makes me miss her more."

Tillie squatted next to her. "If it makes you feel better, my mom is a nice mom."

"I know. Daddy and I talked about her."

"What did he say?"

"He figured us out—only he thought we were trying to get them together because I wanted a new mom instead of us wanting to be sisters. Silly, huh?"

"Why is that silly? If they get married, my mom would be your mom, just like your dad would be my dad." Tillie's wistful tone made Ginnie pause.

She locked her eyes on Tillie. "Do you want my dad to be your dad?"

Tillie looked away. "Sure. I mean, of course. He's nice."

Something about the way Tillie wouldn't look at her annoyed Ginnie. "Do you want him to be your dad more than me to be your sister?"

Tillie glanced at her, then started picking up eggs. "Of course not. You're my best friend. I-I am an only child. I want a sister." She added some eggs to the basket. "*You* have a brother."

Leaning back on her heels, Ginnie couldn't shake being irritated. *Daddy was right. Tillie does want him to be her dad.*

Ginnie shrugged, trying to figure out why it bugged her so much.

Because she wants him more than me. "He told me he wouldn't date her if I didn't want him to."

Panic filled Tillie's eyes. She darted them to Ginnie and then away. *She does want him more.*

"W-what did you tell him?"

Ginnie forced her voice to be friendly. "That I don't need a mom. I have Vi."

Tillie looked like she was going to be sick.

Part of her took small delight in Tillie's reaction. But the more she watched Tillie squirm like a fish on a hook, the more disgusted she became with herself that she would be so mean to her best friend. *Well, she lied, didn't she?*

"You were mad at me yesterday, weren't you?" Tillie whispered.

"No, just confused. Now I'm not." Ginnie couldn't make the hard edge to her voice go away. She wanted to say something nicer, more reassuring, but she couldn't.

Tillie's lip trembled.

You're a lousy friend, Ginnie West. "Why do you like my dad so much?"

"I-I don't. I mean, he's nice and all." Tillie glanced at the door.

Ginnie willed herself to stop, but the words kept coming. "Yes you do. But *why*? He's smothering and strict and he's afraid of letting me be like my mom. He's all happy she was a trick rider but he threatened to sell Calliope if I even try. That's not fair."

"Just because he doesn't want you to get hurt, doesn't make him not fair. At least your dad loves you, Virginia West." Tillie scrambled to her feet and put her hands on her hips. "That's more than *my* dad does." She burst into tears and ran to the door.

Ginnie jumped to her feet. "I'm sorry, Tillie. I don't know why I was being so mean."

"I don't know either. You have *everything!*" Her voice shrilled. "You've got a brother and a horse and Uncle Ben and Uncle Jake and Vi and Buzz. And a yard and ... and ... chickens!" She kicked at two hens flapping close to her feet. "I *only* have a mom. Why is it so wrong to want a dad who'll love me? Yours is the best and *you don't even know it.*"

Tears streamed down Tillie's cheeks. She dropped her face into her hands and sobbed.

All the mad in Ginnie turned to disgust and anger at her big mouth. "I'm sorry. I don't know why I said those things. I'm a horrible sister and friend."

"You aren't usually."

Ginnie cringed. "I know. I was jealous and it was stupid."

Tillie lowered her hands. "Jealous of *me? Why?*"

"Maybe not jealous. Hurt. I thought you liked my dad more than me. And ..."

"And what?" Tillie jutted her chin.

Ginnie swallowed. "I was dumb. I really thought OSS was just about being sisters. Then Dad said the reason we were having him and your mom get together was so I could have a new mom. I didn't want a new mom. I wanted *my* mom."

"My mom's cool!" Tillie protested.

"I know. And I love your mom, but I don't *need* a mom." Ginnie whirled toward the back wall. "Everything's all mixed up."

"So you told him not to date her?"

Ginnie shook her head. "I told him to *marry* her."

"Really?"

Ginnie nodded.

"What did he say?" Tillie licked her lips.

"That he wants to date her and see how that goes because she might not like him."

Tillie smiled. "She likes him alright."

"How do you know?"

"Because she's happier with him around. She's always wanted a nice family. Her father was like my father. *Mean.*" Tillie wiped her cheeks with the back of her hand. "Are we still friends?"

"Yah, *duh.* Forgive me?"

Tillie nodded.

"I'm kinda bummed OSS is over." Ginnie sighed and then smiled. "But I have a secret."

"What?"

"Help me finish and I'll show you."

43

GINNIE SHARES HER SECRET

ow, Gin! That's so cool you found your mom's journals." Tillie ran her finger down a blue stripe. "What did your dad say?"

"I didn't tell him. He's weird about her. I'm going to read them all and then tell him I found them. Like Uncle Jake says, sometimes it's easier to ask forgiveness than for permission."

Tillie's eyes popped open. "I don't know Ginnie. That seems pretty sneaky. He showed you her scrapbook. He'll probably let you read her journals."

"When I asked him about his first date with Mama, he freaked." Ginnie snatched the book from Tillie. "He isn't going to tell me everything, but Mama will."

"Like what?"

Ginnie grinned mischievously. "Like when Mama threatened to shoot him—with a real gun."

"Why?"

"'Cause he snuck in their bedroom to surprise her. She thought he was a burglar and ended up surprising *him* instead."

Tillie giggled. "No way!"

"Yes way. Check it out." Ginnie flipped to the journal entry and read it to Tillie.

"Wow!" Tillie fell back on the bed laughing a minute before sitting up. "I wonder if he'd do that with *my* mom? Good thing she doesn't have a gun."

"I doubt it." Ginnie closed the journal, feeling protective of her dad all of a sudden.

"Does Toran know?"

"Not yet. And you can't tell him."

"Do you think he should know? She's his mom too."

Panic gripped Ginnie. "Tillie, I only trusted you because I was mean to you. You're my best friend and you're probably gonna be my sister. But I need to have this time with my mom all to myself for a while." She set the book on her bed and held Tillie's hands tight.

"I understand."

She shook her head. "No, you don't. You have a mom." Ginnie swallowed a growing lump in her throat. "I'm never going to be able to just sit down and talk to her. So this is sorta my way to just chat with her ... like you do with your mom. If you tell my dad or Toran, that will be ruined. Promise me you won't tell. If you do, we might not be able to be friends anymore."

"Ginnie!"

"I mean it, Tillie!" Ginnie jumped to her feet. "You *can't* tell."

Tillie stood and wrapped her arms firmly around Ginnie.

Ginnie stiffened, regretting she'd shared her secret treasure.

"Cross my heart," Tillie whispered in her ear. "I won't tell. I promise."

Wanting to believe her friend, Ginnie nodded. *You better not.*

44

DAD PREPARES FOR HIS DATE

Ginnie glanced around Dad's room, smiling when she noted his perfectly made bed and Uncle Jake's quickly thrown together one. Everything her dad owned was placed neatly in its designated spot. Uncle Jake's ... not so much. His dresser held a jumble of items including a quart of oil and a stack of papers as well as his shaving kit, while Dad's held a plate for his pocket change, his shaving kit and a bottle of cologne.

Knowing they had shared this room since they were kids, Ginnie often wondered how her neatnik dad could stand living with not-so-tidy Uncle Jake. When she asked him, he grimaced and said something about brotherly love being thicker than water. Since Dad always made sure Toran and her rooms were clean before granting privileges, she decided 'brotherly love' must be some pretty strong stuff.

"Mmm, you smell good." Ginnie inhaled another whiff of Dad's cologne. "Did Mama like this scent?"

He nodded, then looked away. "Yeah, it was her favorite."

"Maybe you should try something different for your new wife?" Ginnie teased.

"Hey, we're just dating." Dad straightened his royal blue tie and looked into his dresser mirror. "I may be a stick-in-the-mud according to you and Jake, but why mess with something that works?"

"I dunno, just to spice things up?"

He grimaced. "I prefer tried-and-true. One thing I like about Amanda is that she's steady."

Yeah, you don't have to worry about her trying to shoot you. Ginnie giggled.

"What's so funny?"

Ginnie shrugged. "You said you were happy with Mama, but from what I can tell, she's like completely opposite of Miss Amanda. Do you think you can be happy with someone so much like you, when Mama was so different?

He took her face in his hand and squeezed gently. "Yes, and that's exactly why."

"I don't get it."

"Because they're so different, there's no need to compare." He sighed. "I loved your mom, so very much. She was energetic and courageous and spontaneous and I loved that—well, sometimes. Sometimes it made me nuts." He winked and chucked her under the chin. "But it was always interesting. Amanda is sweet and kind and she's easy to be around. And I like that, too."

"Isn't it kinda boring?"

"Nope. It's safe."

Ginnie crinkled her face. "Daddy! That is *the* most *unromantic* answer ever. If I were Miss Amanda, I'd kick you to the curb."

"Then it's a good thing you aren't her." He slid his wallet into his back pocket. "Besides, she likes that in me, too. Believe it or not, not everyone craves excitement all the time like you and your mama. Sometimes it's nice to just sit on the front porch swing and simply enjoy the breeze."

"Hmm. Sounds boring."

He chuckled. "It's not. Uncle Ben's taking Toran to a scout meeting and Vi's taking Tillie out wedding dress shopping. Uncle Jake wants to take you out to dinner. Be good, okay?"

"Do I have to go?"

He stared at her. "You'd rather go with Vi? I'm okay with that." He ran his comb through his blond waves. "Vi thought she'd let Tillie help her pick a few bridesmaid dresses for you guys to choose from since you hate dress shopping so much. But if you want to go too, that'll be fine."

Ginnie shook her head. "No, I mean I want to stay home."

"By yourself? What're you wanting to do?"

Read Mama's journals, duh. "Ride Calliope?"

"Not without anybody else home."

"I'm not a baby."

He smiled. "You're *my* baby."

"Not if you adopt Tillie. Then *she'll* be your baby. She's eleven days younger than me."

"You'll always be my baby, no matter what happens." He tugged a braid. "And no, you can't stay by yourself." He took one last look in the mirror, smiled, then straightened up. "What do you think Tillie wants for her birthday?"

"A trip to the mall." Ginnie tapped her cheek and grinned. "Or even better, her own horse."

"A trip to the mall it is." Dad slipped the comb into his pocket. "*She'd* probably love a new dress."

"She'd *really* love a horse."

"A horse is a huge gift." Dad crooked his finger at her and walked to his bedroom door. "And not one I can give to anyone else. I don't always like having the one we have."

"Why not? Calliope's awesome."

"Because." He blew out a breath as they entered the hallway. "You saw your mom's scrapbook, right?"

"So?"

"So, you look like your mother and Calliope looks like hers." He stared out the front window in the hallway, the one that faced their lane. "Sometimes I see you riding and I expect your mom to come breezing through the door. And she doesn't." He stopped talking and inhaled a slow breath. "Sometimes it's all I can do not to whisk you off Calliope's back and hold you, so I know you'll never get hurt like she did. I know I shouldn't, but I want to."

Ginnie took a step back from him. "Are you really that afraid I'll get hurt?"

"Sometimes." He shrugged. "I remind myself that fear and faith can't reside in the same place, but after what happened to your mom, it's hard not to consider that the same thing could happen to you." He placed a firm hand on her shoulder. "I couldn't go through that again. I only got through it the first time because I had to—for you and Toran."

Ginnie smiled. "I'm sure Tillie would love a new dress."

Dad laughed and squeezed her into a hug. "Have fun with Uncle Jake."

45

THE FABULOUS 50'S DINER

$\mathcal{A}$s they entered The Fabulous Fifties Diner, Uncle Jake bopped his way to the working juke box, rocking to Buddy Holly's 'Peggy Sue'. Ginnie laughed when he offered her his hand, twirling her into the booth next to the music box.

Pictures of Elvis, Howdy Doody, The Platters, James Dean, and Chuck Berry hung on the walls with shadow boxes engraved with their names in big letters below them.

A waitress with bright pink lipstick strutted their way, wearing a white blouse, poodle skirt, and an oversized name tag that said 'Betty.'

"Well hey, Darlin'. What can I get for you?" She cracked her gum while jabbing Uncle Jake playfully.

"What's good tonight?" he asked.

"Ohhh, honey, *me*. But since I'm not available, how's about catfish or chicken fried steak? They come with fries or mashed potatoes. We make'em just like your mama used to, skins 'n all."

Uncle Jake smiled. "My niece wants a Frankie and Annette double cheeseburger with Elvis fries. I'm thinking about Minnie Pearl's chicken fried steak and mashed potatoes, though my mama peeled ours."

"Really?" Ginnie liked learning about Grandma.

He nodded. "We'd also like chocolate malts."

"Two chocolate malts coming right up!" Betty picked up their menus and swished away.

The juke box started playing 'Earth Angel' by The Temptations. Uncle Jake grinned. "Hey, that's one of Aunt Sadie's favorite songs. Uncle Ben used to sing it to her. I walked in on him once serenading her in the kitchen. Talk about awkward."

Ginnie giggled and leaned forward. "Tell me about Grandma and Aunt Sadie. Were they good moms?"

"They were both excellent moms to your dad and me. They were also best friends. We'd drive up and spend at least one weekend a month at the farm." Uncle Jake stripped the paper from a straw. "After Grandma died, Aunt Sadie kept me even when I gave her every reason to toss me out."

"Why would you be mean to Aunt Sadie?"

He shook his head. "I wasn't the brightest bulb in the Wests' string of Christmas lights. I was angry when my folks died and took it out on Uncle Ben. Sometimes I let my anger bleed over to Aunt Sadie." Uncle Jake winked at her. "But not often, Uncle Ben made sure of that. He put up with a lot of my nonsense, but not messing with his honey."

"And he shouldn't. Mama says she loved Aunt Sadie and that she couldn't ask for a better 'auntie-mother-in-law'." Ginnie giggled conspiratorially. "She also said she'd make sure she and Daddy stayed happily married because she couldn't give up Uncle Ben and Aunt Sadie."

"You remember Queenie saying that?"

Betty appeared with their malts. "Dinner will be right up." She jabbed Uncle Jake and left.

Ginnie stuffed a big scoop of malt in her mouth. "Yummy. Thanks, Uncle Jake."

"You didn't answer my question." He cleared his throat. "You remember Queenie saying that?"

"Not *saying* it exactly."

"Okay. Then *what* exactly?"

She swallowed slowly. "I don't want to tell you."

"Noted. Tell me anyway."

Ginnie shook her head. "Can we please drop it?"

"I don't think so." Uncle Jake scooped a spoonful of malt.

"Do you promise not to tell my dad?"

"No."

She rolled her eyes. "It isn't bad. I just don't want him to know right now."

"Then tell me."

"No."

Uncle Jake leaned closer and lowered his voice. "Ginnie, if you don't tell me, I'm going to have to presume the worst and let *him* deal with you."

Fury fizzed through her body. "You're not my dad! You don't get to boss me."

"Seriously?" He pointed his spoon at her. "You really want to go there?"

Ginnie considered her options.

Navigating the choppy waters of her dad's anger was one thing, but sailing into the not-so-chartered waters of Uncle Jake's ire was something else. She searched his face. His eyes offered sympathy. "I'm doing this under protest."

"Understood."

"I found my mom's journals. She said she loves Aunt Sadie."

Uncle Jake smiled, leaned back, and raised a questioning brow. "Where's the part you don't want your dad to know?"

"The part where I'm reading her journals. I don't want him to freak out and take them."

"I don't think he'd have a problem with you reading her journals. She *is* your mom."

"But he might."

"And he might not."

"He's weird about Mama." Anxiety threatened to overwhelm her.

Her voice rose like the whistle of their tea kettle. "Her journal is the only way I'm going to get to know Mama *from her*."

"Simmer down, Trouble. This is me, your bud. Chillax."

Ginnie swallowed her rising panic. "I'm reading her pregnancy journal. She found out we're twins, and Daddy knows we're boy and girl twins, but Mama's betting we're both boys."

Uncle Jake chuckled. "Everybody but your dad was surprised when they found out you were a girl."

Betty came back with their dinners and set them on the table with a clunk. Her lips were now ruby red instead of bright pink. She offered Ginnie ketchup and Uncle Jake an exaggerated wink. "Have a nice supper. Please let me know if you need something."

Uncle Jake nodded. "Thank you."

Ginnie squirted ketchup on her plate and picked up a fry. "Mama thought he was going to name me 'Eliza' and Toran either 'Cody' or 'Jared'."

Uncle Jake laughed, then stopped in mid-chuckle. "You know Gin, this should be your dad's call. He should read them and then share them with you, *if* he wants to share."

"No!" Ginnie pointed a fry at him, splattering him with ketchup. "I thought you understood. I *need* to read them."

He frowned and reached for a napkin. "I do understand. But what if she wrote about a fight they might have had? Or something romantic? She's not here, but *he* is and it might embarrass your dad."

Ginnie took a bite of cheeseburger. "Like when she threatened to shoot him 'cause she thought he was a burglar?"

"Yeah." He nodded and then smiled knowingly. "She wrote about *that* in her journal?"

"Yes. Daddy would never tell me that, but Mama did."

"Which is *exactly* my point." Uncle Jake snitched a French fry and dipped it in his gravy. "That was funny—well, not to him when it happened, but still."

"He shouldn't have snuck up on her."

"That's not the point. Todd should decide if you read anything else like that." He slurped a sip of malt and grinned. "*Is* there anything else in her journals like that?" He shook his head. "Wait, don't tell me. That wouldn't be right. If I were him, I wouldn't want my kid reading that kinda thing. He should get a say."

"*Uncle Jake.*"

"Don't 'Uncle Jake' me. You know I have a hard time being the responsible grown-up with you, but this time, I gotta put your dad first. No hard feelings."

"Too late!" Ginnie jumped to her feet. "If you tell and he takes them, we're done being buds."

"He's my brother."

"And I'm you're niece. *You* aren't supposed to be one of the grown-ups." Ginnie snatched a French fry, threw it at him, and stormed off.

"Hey! Come back here!"

She marched into the girls' bathroom.

He followed her to the door. "Virginia! I'm staying right here until you come out!"

"It's going to be a long wait!" Ginnie muttered as she looked in the mirror. "Yeah, Tillie. You want to be part of my family so much. That would include Uncle Jake. He just ditched me for Dad. Some family." She ran some water on a paper towel and then patted her face, blinking rapidly.

"Trouble, could you please hurry?" Uncle Jake called when a lady left the room.

Ginnie walked to the door. "I don't want to talk to you."

"We can't fix this if you don't."

The bathroom door opened again. Another woman left.

Uncle Jake caught the door. "Ma'am, is anyone in there besides my niece?"

"I didn't see anyone."

"Thank you, and excuse me." Uncle Jake walked in the restroom.

"Hey! You can't come in here!"

"Watch me!" He picked her up, tossed her over his shoulder, grabbed her firmly behind her knees, and dashed out the door as quickly as he came in. Dropping some money on the table, he was out the front door in a flash, with Ginnie pounding on his back. "Lemme down!"

"In a minute!" He opened the passenger door of his truck and dropped her on the seat.

Furious, Ginnie kicked her legs as hard as she could.

"Stop!" He held her legs still.

"Let go!"

"When you get yourself under control!"

"I hate you!" Ginnie screamed.

"I love you enough to let you!" He slammed the door shut and leaned against it.

Ginnie darted across the bench of his truck to escape out the driver's door. Uncle Jake opened the passenger door and grabbed her feet, pulling her close.

"No!"

"Stop it!" He grasped each of Ginnie's arms and pushed her roughly against the back of the seat. "Virginia Maie! I have never raised a hand to you, but if you don't stop, that's gonna change!"

The sternness of his tone made her freeze. She glared at him and then looked away.

"Are you going to stay?"

"Yes, sir!" she snapped.

"Good! Simmer down and let's talk."

She jutted her chin. "There's nothing to talk about. I shouldn't have trusted you."

"Change of plans! *I* talk, *you* don't. You're just being spiteful."

"So tell my dad!" She crossed her arms. "You're going to anyway!"

"What part of '*you don't talk*' don't you understand? Nobody said you couldn't read the journals. I just think your dad has a right to preview ones that pertain to *him*." Uncle Jake relaxed his hold.

Ginnie freed her arms. "What if he won't let me read *any* of them? I need them!"

He pressed the lock. "Stay put!" He closed her door, rushed around the front of the cab, opened his door, and slid onto the bench seat.

"I don't hate you," Ginnie whispered.

"I know."

"I didn't even want to come. I wanted to stay home and read Mama's journal." Ginnie buried her face in her hands. "You're going to tell my dad I went nuts and he'll take them."

"I'll talk to him so he doesn't, okay?"

She blinked away hot tears and folded her arms. "That's not a promise you can keep."

"I'll make him understand. I've never failed you. We can still be buds."

"Unless Daddy takes away the journals."

"You're harsh."

"Then make him understand."

"I will." Uncle Jake turned the engine key and backed out of his parking space.

Ginnie blinked rapidly, slamming her fist against the door.

46

HOME

*G*innie's steps echoed on the gray concrete as she followed Uncle Jake up the front porch stairs and through the front door. She blinked at the light flooding from the chandelier in the entryway, momentarily pausing the flurry of thoughts bouncing around inside her mind.

Glancing around the foyer, she fixed her gaze on the family photos lining both sides of the extra wide hallway. Inspiration slapped her upside the head. "How about *you* preview the journals? Then I won't have to tell Daddy."

Uncle Jake shook his head. "She was Todd's wife. I couldn't do that."

"Please?" Ginnie hopes sank.

Uncle Jake's jaw tightened. "No, and drop it before I have to pull the 'adult card' on you. Neither one of us likes me when you make me do that."

Ginnie rolled her eyes. "Yes, sir! Whatever you say, *sir*."

"Knock it off."

"Can I just go to my room?"

"Good idea. Get ready for bed and brush your teeth."

She headed for the stairs. "You promised you'd make him understand so I can keep the journals." Ginnie stopped on the fourth step and looked him straight in the eye. "You're going to *keep* that promise, right?"

Her sarcasm didn't go over well.

"When have I ever lied to you? Just go." He jerked his thumb at the stairs. "I'm trying to figure out how to tell Todd you threw a huge temper tantrum in a very public place, and convince him not to ground you for the rest of your life. One thing at a time."

His frustration opened the flood gates of emotions she had been holding in check the whole ride home. Ginnie threw her hands up. "*You* embarrassed *me*. *You* were wrong. Not *me*."

The study door opened. Uncle Ben appeared. "What's all this yelling about?"

Uncle Jake ignored Uncle Ben, strode over to the bottom step, meeting Ginnie eye-to-eye. "Maybe I won't try so hard to keep you out of trouble. I'll let your dad know what happened and let *you* deal with the fallout."

Furious, Ginnie's hands flew to her hips. "You shouldn't have been in a woman's bathroom!" Even as the words crossed her lips, she knew her dad would take Uncle Jake's side.

"I wouldn't have had to if you'd been reasonable and just talked to me."

"I asked you a question," Uncle Ben reminded them and then pointed a finger at Uncle Jake. "And why on earth would you go into a woman's restroom? What were you thinking?"

Uncle Jake jerked his thumb at Ginnie. "Ask her. She went all psycho on me."

When Uncle Ben cleared his throat at Uncle Jake, Ginnie made a pitch for her great-uncle's sympathy. "Uncle Jake lied to me."

"About what?" Uncle Jake's words oozed with confidence. "I told you I wouldn't go around your dad when you first brought it up." He shook his head at Uncle Ben. "I didn't lie."

Uncle Ben crooked his finger at Ginnie. "What happened?"

Ginnie stood still. "Can I just go to my room? Please?"

Uncle Ben shook his head. "This needs to be resolved first. Jake, what happened?"

"She found Queenie's journals. Being the responsible big brother that I–*on occasion*–try to be–I told my *niece* that her dad should read them first and then share with her what he thinks she should know."

"When did you find Mama's journals?"

Ginnie jutted her head upward to where Toran leaned over the rails. "And why wouldn't you tell *me*? You're some kind of sister. And my twin, no less. Thanks a lot ... you traitor."

"Victor West, there's no need for name calling. I'm sure Ginnie has a good reason for not sharing your mother's journals with you." Uncle Ben arched a warning eyebrow. "One which she'll do well to share ... quickly."

Ginnie crossed her arms across her chest and dropped onto the step behind her. She glanced at Toran's betrayed look, and then glared at Uncle Jake. "You've ruined everything! Why couldn't you just leave it alone? This is why I didn't want to tell you. I take it back. I *do* hate you!"

Uncle Jake's mouth dropped open.

"Ginnie, you don't mean that." Uncle Ben was in front of her in two quick strides. He held up his hand at Uncle Jake when he started to respond. "Don't."

Uncle Ben looked up at Toran. "Come down here please." And then motioned for Ginnie to stand.

Ginnie debated about obeying just long enough to catch a warning in Uncle Jake's eye. "Now!" he mouthed.

She swallowed and stood.

Light shined in the screen door as Dad pulled into his parking spot.

"Great. Your dad finally goes on a date for the first time in years and he comes home to *this* mess." Uncle Jake shook his head and gave a disgusted whistle. "Just dandy."

47
DAD FINDS OUT

*C*W hy do I get the feeling I should've stayed out?" Dad glanced at each family member. When no one made an attempt to answer him, his gaze landed on Ginnie. "Should I be diplomatic and ask for somebody, *anybody* to volunteer some information? Or should I just take a stab in the dark and ask what leading role *you've* played in tonight's drama?"

"Very funny." Ginnie squelched the urge to roll her eyes. "But this is *Uncle Jake's* fault."

Her uncle's eyebrows scrunched together. "In what universe?"

"He was my *second* choice." Dad shot Ginnie a warning look and turned to his brother.

"Yeah, because Toran couldn't possibly be at fault." Ginnie crossed her arms again and glared. "Because *he's* perfect."

Dad raised a warning finger. "Do you hear that?"

"Hear what?"

"That huge cracking sound." He steeled his gaze on her. "It's the sound of you stepping on *very* thin ice. Keep it up and you're grounded."

Ginnie clamped her jaw shut, then ground her teeth when Uncle Jake snorted.

"Sorry, but that was pretty good." He winked at Dad. "Very fatherly. Or Uncle Ben-ish."

Uncle Ben cleared his throat. "Jake, maybe you and I should go for a walk. Todd's very capable of handling his own kids."

If she wasn't so mad at him, Ginnie might have laughed when Uncle Jake grinned and raised his hands, miming surrender.

One look at Dad's aggravated face and she was even more frustrated. Dad pointed at the living room and stepped out of her way. Swallowing hard, Ginnie walked past him, casting a pleading look at her brother.

Toran shook his head and followed her into the living room.

Uncle Jake and Uncle Ben brought up the rear of their little caravan.

When Ginnie and Toran sat on the couch and met Dad's gaze, he raked his fingers through his hair and then plunged his hand into his pocket. "Just so you know, I had a great time with Amanda tonight and came home in a wonderful mood. I'd really like to enjoy that feeling. So, before we start, let me make this easy for you. I'll ask what happened and you answer with as little drama and attitude as possible and we'll move through this quickly. Do that and I'll try not to ground you for the rest of your life, okay?"

Dad's attempt at humor did little to soothe Ginnie's anger. *Tillie should see you now. Then I bet she wouldn't think you're such a cool dad. This is all Uncle Jake's fault and I'm the one getting lectured.*

She sifted through the thoughts tumbling in her mind like a whacked out game of Fifty-two Pickup, hoping to find an explanation that would gain Dad's sympathy.

Finally, she settled on telling the truth and hoped that would fix this mess. "I found Mama's journals and started reading one. Uncle Jake made me tell him. And then he said I had to tell you. I told him I didn't want you to know because you might take them away from me."

When Dad's mouth opened in surprise, Ginnie added quickly, hoping for sympathy. "When I went into the *women's* restroom to calm down, he came in and got me. Then threw me in his truck and brought me home."

"I didn't exactly throw you."

"Yes, you did." Ginnie glared at her uncle and then turned to her dad. "And he threatened to hit me."

Dad jerked his head toward Uncle Jake.

"She kicked me. Over and over again."

"Did you really kick him?" Dad asked.

Ginnie tapped her foot. "He deserved it. *He lied.*"

"Stop saying that, I didn't lie." Uncle Jake wagged a scolding finger. "I told you I wouldn't go around your dad." He stepped toward Dad. "I had your back, Todd. Queenie wrote about the time she almost shot you *and* about Cody."

Dad took a step back and reached for the window sill, like he needed to steady himself.

"Mama shot you?" Toran leaned forward. "And who's Cody?"

"*Almost* shot him," Ginnie corrected and then continued to glare at Uncle Jake. She twisted toward her brother. "*You* were Cody. Well, I might've been Cody, but I wasn't a boy."

Toran looked at her liked she'd grown a third eyeball. "What are you talking about?"

"Mama wanted to name us Cody and Jared, but she didn't." Ginnie turned to Dad. "Why didn't she? I mean I know why she didn't name me either of those, but you didn't name me Eliza like you told her you wanted too. Why not?"

Ginnie stopped talking when she noticed Dad gazing long and hard at Uncle Ben.

"Todd, it seems like a good time to tell them." Uncle Ben placed a hand on Dad's shoulder. "Unless you want me too."

Dad shook his head and lowered his voice. "They should hear this from me."

"Sorry, man. I didn't mean for this to happen." Uncle Jake dropped into the dark blue armchair. "I had hoped to distract Ginnie and give you a head's up. Things got out of control. I'm really sorry."

"I see how that could've happened." Dad moved the coffee table back a little and then sat on it as he glanced from Ginnie to Toran. "This isn't how I wanted you to find out, but that can't be helped now."

He blew out a quiet breath and looked at Uncle Ben, who gave an encouraging nod.

48

CODY

*D*ad stood. He paced the length of the room before he sat down again. "Cody didn't end up being either one of you. But he did exist. He was your little brother." Dad glanced between them and then whispered. "He died."

Ginnie fell back against the couch and exchanged puzzled looks with Toran.

"We were triplets?" Toran asked.

"No." Dad shook his head. "Your mom was twenty-two weeks pregnant with him when *she* died."

Toran leaned forward. "Why didn't you save him?"

"He was too little." Dad swallowed hard. "He couldn't have lived outside of her body."

Ginnie licked her lips. "W-why didn't you tell us before?"

"You knew at the time, but forgot because you were so young." Dad rubbed his slacks. "When you stopped asking about Cody, I was okay with that. It was easier for me. And there never seemed to be a good reason to remind you."

All the anger in Ginnie deflated like a popped balloon as she processed the news. She sought out Toran's hand and squeezed. "I'm

193

sorry, Daddy. Mama didn't mention that, but she's pregnant with *us* in the journal I'm reading."

He placed a hand on each of their knees. "She liked the name Cody, but we went with Victor Alexander for Toran because she wanted to give both of our dads a namesake. She liked the nickname 'Toran' and pulled it out of both names. We planned to have at least six kids. So, she figured a different son could be Cody, and he was."

Ginnie and Toran looked at each other, and then together, leaned toward Dad. He enveloped one in each arm and held tight. Ginnie's mind went blank like a freshly washed blackboard, wanting to offer words of comfort to all of them, but didn't know what to say.

Dad continued. "And I was so in love with your mom that I wanted to name *you* after her. If you know about Eliza, then you know about our agreement." He released them.

Toran looked from Ginnie to Dad. "What agreement?"

Remembering Mama's words, Ginnie laughed softly in spite of the sad news. "You do realize that she only agreed to that because she thought we were both boys?"

Dad nodded and then offered a mischievous smile, seeming relieved to change the subject. "It doesn't matter because like you said, I *knew* you were a girl. If I didn't, I would have suggested we each get to name one of you anyway."

"That's a bit sneaky, don't you think?" she asked.

His smile reminded her of the Cheshire cat. "I learned from the best. Your mom was awesome at thinking outside the box and getting her way. I beat her at her own game, for once." Dad stopped smiling and leveled her with a penetrating gaze. "And speaking of sneaky, when did you find her journals and *why* didn't you tell me?"

"I didn't sneak." Ginnie threw up her hands, frustration creeping back. "Princess hid her babies in the loft and they all meowed. I wanted to make sure they were okay. She ran off by Mama's stuff."

"So why didn't you tell me you found them?"

"Or me?" Toran added.

"I was going to, as soon as I finished reading the journals." Ginnie turned to Toran. "You have your new computer. I miss her and she writes like she's having a conversation, like she knows it's me, at least sometimes." She glanced at Dad. "I don't want you to take them away. I *need* them."

He jiggled his knee and looked at Uncle Ben. After a few seconds, Dad pulled her onto his lap and hugged her tight. "Where are the journals?"

She hesitated, then whispered, "One's in my room."

"Okay. Why don't you and Toran get ready for bed and the three of us will read that one together. I'd like to see what she has to say and I think Toran has a right to know what you know."

Toran nodded. "Yeah, me too."

Ginnie's heart raced. "But I can keep them? And read them?"

"Keep? *No.* Read? *Yes.*" He helped her stand. "I'll be up in a minute." He reached for Toran to hug him and then stopped. "Did you really kick Uncle Jake?"

After glancing at her uncle, who gave a friendly wink, she smiled at Dad. "Yah, but it's all good now. Right, Uncle Jake?"

"It's okay, Todd. Trouble and I worked it out."

"Okay, *this once.*" Dad gripped her arm firmly. "*But ... just ... this once.*" Ginnie swallowed. "Yes, sir."

"I'll be up in a minute." The words dripped with warning.

Turning to her brother, she and Toran exchanged startled looks. Ginnie offered a silent prayer that Uncle Ben and Uncle Jake would put Dad back in a gentler mood before he came upstairs.

She swallowed hard and hurried from the room.

49

READING THE JOURNALS

$\mathcal{A}$fter Ginnie changed into her pajamas, she paced with the pink-and-blue journal in her arms. Her belly growled. She remembered the yummy cheeseburger and fries that got left at the diner. Even though she was hungry, Ginnie didn't dare go downstairs.

Knowing Uncle Jake, he would probably do his best to put Dad in a better mood about their fight. As far as she could recall, she'd never been so angry with Uncle Jake in her entire life. Certainly she'd never been angry enough to kick him.

She knew her dad expected her to obey Uncle Jake like any other adult in the home, but it never felt the same as say, having to mind Uncle Ben.

There was a knock at the door.

She whirled around. "Come in."

Toran appeared in his blue pj's printed with assorted sports balls. "Is that her journal?"

Ginnie looked down. "Yeah. The one I'm reading."

He crossed the room and reached for it.

Instead of handing it over, she walked to her bed and set her pillows against the headboard, so it looked like a couch. After crawling across the bed, she sat against a pillow. "I want you to read something." She searched for the passage where Mama found out she was pregnant with twins and handed the journal to her brother. She watched his eyes zip back and forth across the pages.

A reverent look crossed her twin's face. He smiled. "She really wanted us, didn't she?"

"Of course she did. *I* told you that.(this sounds more like Ginnie's voice than Todd's)" Dad stood in the doorway, shaking his head. In four steps, he was next to them.

"She called us miracles," Ginnie said.

"Because you were and are. We wanted *each* of you, very much."

Toran looked up. "It's nice to hear it from Mama as well."

"I'm sure it is. Ginnie, where did you leave off?"

"Mama's going to find out that I'm a girl."

He smiled. "Her face was priceless. She was so sure you were both boys." Dad took off his boots and set them next to her bed. "Start there and go forward. Between us, we can fill Toran in if he has any questions."

Ginnie traded spots with Toran so she could be in the middle. Once each of them got comfortable, Ginnie found where she left off. "How did you know I was a girl?"

"I just knew. Inspiration happens differently for each person. One day, your mom had a feeling you needed her. She came into your room just as you started to climb over the railing of the crib and caught you before you hit the ground." He gave a soft laugh. "Knowing you were a girl was a special secret I had with you and God. It was cool. And when she found out I was right, she was *really* impressed. That made it even cooler."

Toran leaned forward. "Did you have any secrets about me?"

"I knew you were a boy."

"Well, duh. That's a no-brainer. We have twenty-seven boy cousins in our generation." Toran shook his head. "A *special* secret."

"Only three are older, though." Dad rubbed his chin. "I knew when I saw you that you were an old soul in a new body. That you would always challenge the way I think about things and you do."

Toran relaxed against the headboard. "That's not the same, but I can live with it."

"Good. Ginnie, start reading."

Ginnie leaned against Dad. "Okay then. Mama says she had a bad night and you were kind enough to rub her back until she felt better. And then she started craving double fudge sundaes, with roasted pecans, three cherries, whipped topping and a jalapeño pepper. Ick. And did she really want jalapeños on her sundae?"

Dad nodded, smiling. "She sure did. She didn't like pickles—even pregnant. But she loved jalapenos—dipped in hot fudge."

"That actually sounds kinda good," Toran said.

Ginnie shuddered. "Maybe *to you.*"

"I often teased her that you two probably were the reason she came up with such weird combinations. That her cravings were to please each of you. She liked strawberry jam mixed in salsa as well as peanut butter and cheddar on a toasted bagel."

"Yuck," Ginnie said.

"Interesting," Toran mused.

"Of course you'd think so." Shaking her head, Ginnie started reading about the sonogram the next day.

Holy Smokes, Todd was right. Now I have to let him name one.

All three of them laughed.

"When did you decide to name me after Mama?"

"When the doctor confirmed you were a girl."

"And you let her keep thinking I was going to be Eliza?"

"For a while."

Toran chuckled. "That's pretty wicked, Dad."

"No. It was my sense of self-preservation kicking in. You've argued with your sister. Try living with a grown-up Ginnie with whacked out hormones. Angry one minute, in tears the next." Dad shook his head and cleared his throat. "I knew better than to start something that would take months to finish. Once you guys were born, I figured she'd be more open to it and I was right. Keep reading, you'll see."

They laughed a lot and joked a little, enjoying Mama's take on her life and pregnancy. The more they read, the more Dad relaxed. They read until she and Toran were born.

I've been beat up and tired from performing the most excruciating routines. I've been tossed from mechanical bulls and champion stallions, and yet labor was intense in a way I didn't imagine. Todd finally convinced me that an epidural wouldn't hurt the babies and I was glad I finally gave in. It made all the difference in the world.

Dad chuckled. "She was a trooper. Your mama wouldn't ever take more than an ibuprofen. And she never admitted easily she was wrong, but it's nice to know she thought I was right."

Toran pulled the book closer. "Mama's journal feels like a letter from Heaven."

"It does, Toran. I'm glad you found this, Gin."

"Me too." She kept reading.

The coolest and weirdest thing about the experience was that even though I'd just given birth to our perfect little boy, I was still pregnant.

"That would be weird," Ginnie mused.

Dad nodded. "I was really torn after Toran was born. I wanted to count his fingers and toes but Queenie still needed me because *you* were coming." Dad smiled at Toran. "We kissed you and handed you off to a nurse and waited for Ginnie to be born. That was the best. There were no babies and then you came, Toran. And then you, Ginnie. When the family started showing up after you guys were born, nobody had to wait too long to hold a baby." He chucked Ginnie under the chin and laughed. "Although Vi hogged you and Aunt Sadie wouldn't give up Toran." A wistful look crossed his face. "Where are the rest of her journals?"

Ginnie's chest tightened. "Are you going to take them?"

He nodded. "Don't get upset. Where are they?"

"But you said I could read them."

"*After* I read them. Where are they?"

"In the food storage room."

Dad turned to get off the bed.

Ginnie grabbed his hand. "Please don't take them. I need them."

"I won't take them all."

"Promise?"

"Yes."

She led them to Vi's door.

Dad knocked. No answer.

"She's probably still out with Preston." He reached for the knob. "Don't touch anything." He opened the door and they crossed Vi's room to the food room door. Dad opened it and flipped on the light switch. "Go ahead and get them."

Ginnie hesitated and then did as he asked.

Dad took the box from her and reversed their steps.

When they returned to Ginnie's room, Dad set the box of journals on her bed. He browsed through the box, pulling out a bright pink book that said simply, 'Ginnie' on the front. He also fished out a bright blue one that said 'Toran'. After putting the rest of them back in the box, he handed each their book.

"These are for each of you, from your mom. I know she would've liked to have written more, but remember, she was the mother of newborn twins, and her time was limited, okay?"

Ginnie nodded. "Thank you."

"Yeah, Dad. Thanks," Toran added.

"You're welcome." He leaned over and kissed Ginnie goodnight, tickling her forehead. "Do you want me to leave your light on?"

Ginnie nodded.

"Don't stay up too late. You can read tomorrow while I'm at work. Goodnight, honey." He motioned to the door for Toran.

"Goodnight, Daddy." Ginnie held the journal next to her chest, barely remembering to breathe.

50

MORE BAD NEWS

*G*ood morning, Gin! Rise and shine!" Dad opened Ginnie's emerald green curtains.

Ginnie sensed the brightness of the morning sun through her eyelids and squeezed them tighter.

"Morning." Her raspy voice startled her.

"Did you get much sleep?"

Shifting slightly, the pink journal slid off her chest. "I guess."

"We need to hurry with the chores. We all overslept." He jiggled her foot. "You need to get up."

Ginnie yawned, then remembered the journals her dad took last night. She sat up as her eyes sprang open. "Did you read any of Mama's journals?" Ginnie's voice grew with excitement. Dad nodded. "Can I have the ones you read back?"

"Before I answer that, I'd like to ask you something." He sat next to her.

Ginnie nodded, suspicious of his kindness. "Okay."

"These last few days, how open would you say I've been with you about your mom and all?"

"Very open, I guess." Still tired, Ginnie felt like her brain was shuffling through pudding as she tried to figure out where he was

going with the question. "What does that have to do with the journals?" Fully awake now, Ginnie knew this game of twenty questions
would not end well.

Dad cleared his throat and stood. "I need you to give me a pass on
getting the journals back to you."

Ginnie threw back her comforter. "But you promised!"

"I know. I intend to keep that promise, just not right away."

She jerked to her knees, almost losing her balance in her hurry.
"But you already said I could."

"I know, but I need to change that. Can you let me explain?"

Forcing herself to nod, Ginnie slid to the edge of her bed, placing
her fisted hands under her legs.

Dad paced halfway between her bed and the door, and turned.
"I've embraced your mom's memory in a way I haven't in a really long
time." Pausing, he darted his gaze between Ginnie and the window.
"Before I showed you her scrapbook, I kept her memory in a box in
my mind, like a present I could peek at, but not take out and play
with. Does that make sense to you?"

He's not going to let me read them! I shouldn't have told Uncle Jake!

"There are some things I can't share with you right now."

Ginnie jumped to her feet. "But I understood about Cody."

Dad sat down and patted the spot beside him. "I know. But I still
need you to give me some space about the journals. Can you do
that?"

"Do I have a choice?" She sat carefully, hoping her obedience
would change his mind.

"Not really."

Her heart pounded. "How long?"

"I don't know. A while."

"A *long* while?"

Dad sighed.

Hot tears burned her eyes. She turned from him, blinking.

"Gin, I didn't mean to make you cry. I'm sorry."

A lump welled in her throat. "I really want to read those journals." Ginnie exhaled, scrambling to make a bargain he'd agree to. "I won't talk to you about them. I'll just read them."

He shook his head. "Not right now. I'm sorry."

She barely heard the whisper. Ginnie pushed off the bed. "Please?" She grabbed his hand. "Please, give them back. They're all I have of Mama. If you love me, you'll give them back."

"I *do* love you, but I can't give them to you right now. I'm sorry." He pointed to her chest of drawers, his tone offering sympathy. "Get dressed. We have chores."

Ginnie whirled from him. "No, you don't."

"I don't what?"

"Love me." She rubbed her arms. "If you loved me, you'd give them back."

"Look at me."

Ginnie folded her arms defiantly and turned further away.

"I asked you to do something." The firmness of his tone didn't move her. "Virginia Maie, don't make me count. You're too old for this. *Look* at me."

Instinctively, she turned, hating that she couldn't be an unfeeling statue. She steeled her gaze on him, her voice taking on a hard edge. "What?"

His eyes narrowed. "I said I'm sorry. I don't expect you to understand. But please try to respect I have my reasons. I don't want to hurt you, it just can't be helped."

"Yes, it can." She swiveled away from him. "*Mama* would let me read them, I know she would."

He rested a hand on her shoulder. "You don't know that."

She jerked her shoulder from his touch and glared. "Because *you* won't let me get to know her. You don't talk about her. You won't let me be like her. You're an ostrich! You're afraid of everything. I could find out about her *from her* and leave you out of it, but you won't let me. I *hate* you."

His hand flinched.

Ginnie took a step back from him.

He shoved his hand in his pocket. "Are you done? Because I am." He turned and strode to the door.

She rushed after him. "*Please?* I need my mom." She grabbed his work sleeve. "Please, Daddy. Give me the journals back!" Her voice rose higher with each syllable. "If you love me, you will."

He gripped her wrist with his free hand and pried her hand off his. "I can't. I'm sorry."

Ginnie shook her head, refusing to see sympathy in his eyes. "You're *not* sorry. *Not one little bit.* You're a liar. Just like Uncle Jake. He said he'd make you understand. *You don't.*"

"I do." He swiveled, clenching his jaw. "Get dressed. You have five minutes to be downstairs."

"You said you'd give me my mom if you could! You can, *but you won't.*"

He fisted his hands. "Five minutes." He walked out the door, slamming it closed behind him.

51

DONE WITH EVERYBODY

Ginnie charged through Toran's room on her way downstairs, nearly running into Uncle Jake as she turned into the hallway. "Hey, Trouble."

Glaring, she ignored him and rushed toward the stairs.

He caught her hand.

She snatched it back. "I shouldn't have trusted you. You both lied. *Leave. Me. Alone.*"

"Hey!"

Ginnie scrambled down the stairs.

"What did I lie about?"

"He took them." She wiped at angry tears. "And he's not giving them back. I'm done with you both." Spurred by her anger, she flew through the screen door, barely out of his grasp.

He followed on her heels.

Jumping off the porch, she darted between Dad's car and Vi's VW bug. Uncle Jake grabbed her upper arm.

"Let go of me."

"When you work this out with me. He said he'll give them back, so he will."

"Not anymore." She jerked her arm, but he tightened his grip. "He changed his mind. You *promised* I'd get to read them." She kicked his shin. "You've ruined everything."

"Again? I thought you were done kicking! Geez, Trouble." His grasp loosened.

She bolted up the hill.

"Jacob. Let her be." Ginnie barely registered Uncle Ben's words while increasing the distance between them.

"Ginnie, come back! I didn't know."

"Jake, leave it alone. Todd'll deal with her."

The thud of Uncle Jake's boots stopped.

Not if he can't find me, he won't. Ginnie sprinted towards the barn. She snapped on Calliope's lead and led her out of the stall. Giving a quick glance to the saddle, she decided to ride bareback.

Realizing her riding helmet was still in the stall, she decided to leave it. Taking the time to retrieve it would give Dad too much time to catch up to her. She stopped by a bale of hay and mounted her horse.

"If you leave this barn on her, I'll have Calliope sold in a heartbeat."

A tremor coursed through her. She glanced forward.

Dad's body filled the doorway. "Get down."

"I can't have my mom, her journals, *or* my horse?"

"You heard me. I'm counting to two." A finger went up. "One."

"You know riding Calliope calms me. Why can't I?"

He took a step closer, raising a second finger.

She slid off the far side of Calliope.

He took hold of her horse's reins and pointed to a hay bale in the corner. "Stay here." He led the mare back to her stall.

Glaring at his back, Ginnie waited until he disappeared around the corner. Anger and frustration simmered until it boiled over.

She whirled toward the barn door and bolted out of it.

52

BEST DAD? NOT SO MUCH

Sweeping the layout of the farm, Ginnie ran downhill, hoping to get to the other side of the woodshed before Dad could spot her. From there, she could dart to the hay barn and hide in the loft until he left for work. He could ground her until Christmas for all she cared. *Best dad? Not anymore. I'm ripping up that shirt the next time I get my hands on it.*

Ginnie rounded the woodshed. Standing in front of the cars, talking with Uncle Ben, Uncle Jake, and Toran stood Tillie ... and Miss Amanda. *Yes! Miss Amanda will help.*

Dad was just behind her. "Virginia, Stop!"

Not gonna happen.

She bounded down the hill and rushed toward Miss Amanda, only slowing as she flew past her. Ginnie turned quickly and jogged to a stop, throwing her arms around Miss Amanda's waist.

Dad slowed to a walk next to Uncle Jake, pointing a scolding finger. "I told you to stay."

Ginnie peeked out from behind Miss Amanda's back and glared. "You also told me I could read Mama's journals. You *lied*." She buried her face in Miss Amanda's sky blue blouse.

Miss Amanda patted Ginnie's shoulder protectively. "Todd, what's going on?"

"We had a misunderstanding." He blew out an aggravated breath. "Which we can clear up if my daughter will quit throwing a fit and behave reasonably."

Toran took a step toward him. "Dad, you did tell us we could read the journals."

Ginnie swiped furiously at tears she couldn't stop. "He lied."

"Ginnie!" Tillie gasped.

"You want him to be your dad?" Ginnie locked her eyes on Tillie's and then waved her hand angrily at her dad. "You can have him. I don't want him anymore."

"Virginia West, that's enough." Uncle Ben swept a warning finger around the circle, stopping at Ginnie. "Nobody speak unless you can do it civilly."

Miss Amanda pressed Ginnie into a protective hug. "It's okay. We can work this out. Your dad loves you."

Dad hooked a thumb in his pocket. "I'm sorry I hurt you."

Tillie's hand flew to her mouth, her eyes wide.

"I didn't hit her, I hurt her feelings." Dad corrected, glancing from Ginnie to Tillie. "She's fine, or she will be if she'll settle down and let me explain."

Ginnie shook her head and looked at Miss Amanda. "He lied. He won't let me have my mom. He said I could, and then he took her away." She blinked hard. "*I. Need. Her.*"

Unwelcome tears cascaded down her cheeks.

"H-how can he give you your mom?" Miss Amanda raised a questioning eyebrow to Dad.

"Not Queenie *exactly*. She found Queenie's journals." He lifted Ginnie's chin. "I gave you the one your mama wrote for you. Make that be good enough for now."

"Why can't we have the others?" Toran asked.

"Because you can't. Don't you start, too." Dad squeezed Ginnie's chin a little too firmly. "I said I was sorry. I don't expect you to understand, I just ..." Dad glanced at his watch and grimaced. "I can't do this right now. I have to get to work."

"Todd, I'll go and cover for you while you fix things with Ginnie," Uncle Jake offered.

"I wish you could, but I have that meeting with Seb." Dad wiped Ginnie's tears with his thumb. He squatted to her eye level. "I don't want to leave you like this, but I have to go."

Uncle Jake squeezed her shoulder. "Trouble, it'll be okay. Trust me."

"Why should I? You said you'd make him understand." Ginnie wiped at her tears and then made a slashing motion with her hand. "He *doesn't* understand. *Nobody* does."

"I do." Toran gave her shoulder a quick squeeze. "She was *my* mom too." Toran squared his body to Dad's and stood tall. "I hope your reasons are *really* good, Dad, because you're crushing my sister. Nobody gets to hurt her, *even you*."

Ginnie turned toward her twin, double checking that it was Toran standing in front of her.

Frustration flashed across Dad's face, then softened as Toran crossed his arms over his chest.

"I do have good reasons, Tor. Please trust me." Dad placed a firm hand on Toran's shoulder and offered a half-hearted smile. "I'm glad you're so protective of your sister, but try not to make a habit of being defiant. I wouldn't hurt her if I could help it, but I can't."

Ginnie swallowed, waiting for Toran's reply.

"You've never given me a reason to defy you before. Please don't make *that* a habit."

"Fair enough." Dad leaned toward Ginnie and lowered his voice. "I've never lied to you and I won't start now. I just need some time."

When she refused to meet his gaze, he tried again. "I'll make this right as soon as I can."

Although she wanted to make him feel better, she wanted Mama's journals more. She turned away from him.

Miss Amanda hugged her close. "Todd, do what you have to do. I'll see to Ginnie."

Ginnie searched Miss Amanda's face. "You'll stay with me?"

"For as long as you need me."

"Okay." Ginnie stiffened when her dad hugged her.

"Honey, I *am* sorry."

"Can I have the journals back?"

He shook his head.

"Then you're not sorry enough."

"That does it." Dad reached for her arm.

Ginnie stepped back.

"Todd, wait." Miss Amanda held up her hand to Dad, putting herself between them and looked Ginnie in the eye. "Whatever he can't tell you right now must be important. Please give him a hug good-bye. You'll both feel better."

With a quick glance to Tillie, who stood nearby, pale and twirling her hair quickly around her finger, and then to Dad—who shifted his weight from one foot to the other, she gave a quick nod.

Dad pulled her close and kissed the crown of her head. "I do love you." Ginnie couldn't force the same words to her lips.

He walked toward Uncle Jake's truck, watching her the whole time, looking as lost and miserable as she felt.

Miss Amanda rubbed Ginnie's arms encouragingly and whispered. "It'll be okay."

Fresh tears rolled down Ginnie's cheeks.

She shook her head. *No, it won't.*

53

TAILLIGHTS

*A*fter watching the tail lights on Uncle Jake's truck grow smaller and smaller until they disappeared down the lane, Tillie grabbed Ginnie's hand. "I thought you weren't going to tell your dad about the journals?"

"Uncle Jake made me."

"I'm sorry." Tillie's gaze lowered to her sneakers. "I figured he'd let you read them. It shouldn't be such a big deal."

"No kidding." Ginnie wiped her eyes and turned to Toran. "Thanks for sticking up for me."

"I already told you it was: 'Be My Sister's Keeper Day' in Heaven when they paired us as twins." He hitched his thumb at his chest and smiled. "I was right."

Ginnie wiped her tears with her mint green t-shirt sleeve. "I still think it was 'Opposite Day', but I'm glad we got paired up."

"Me too."

She swiveled toward Uncle Ben. "You know why he took them, don't you?"

"I have my suspicions. But *he* needs to tell you. Not me."

"That's not fair."

Her great-uncle narrowed his eyes and pointed to the barn. "We need to finish the chores."

"Talk to Miss Amanda, Gin. Tillie and I'll get the chores done." Toran looked to Uncle Ben, daring him to argue. "Miss Amanda promised to stay until she felt better."

"I was there, Toran." Uncle Ben stood a little taller. "Please see to the hogs."

"Yes, sir," Toran replied crisply, throwing Uncle Ben a look of disgust. "Come on, Tillie."

It took everything Ginnie had not to smile as Uncle Ben clamped his jaw shut.

Wow! Toran's really ticked too.

Uncle Ben exchanged glances and nods with Miss Amanda.

Miss Amanda slipped an arm around Ginnie's shoulders and walked her toward the front porch.

"You know if you marry my dad, Uncle Ben will be kinda like *your* dad." Ginnie cast a long glance to where her Uncle Ben had been and then rolled her eyes.

Miss Amanda chuckled. "Believe it or not, that's a selling point for me. I *love* Uncle Ben."

"I hate it when he and Daddy gang up on me."

"Uncle Ben just tries to be supportive of your dad." They climbed the steps to the front porch. "It's not easy being a single parent. Uncle Ben's been doing it for nine years and your dad for eight. I've been doing it for six. Though in my case, it's easier to be single than married."

After considering several ways to ask, Ginnie just blurted the question on her mind. "Are you going to marry my dad?"

Miss Amanda gestured to the swing. "How do you feel about that?"

"I'm okay with it, but ..." Ginnie locked her gaze on the railing across from them.

"But what?"

"I don't want to hurt your feelings."

"You won't."

Ginnie sat on the swing. "Did my dad tell you about OSS?"

"He mentioned you and Tillie had a scheme to get us together, but you were happier about getting a sister than a mom."

"That's not true." Ginnie slid to her feet. "I just didn't think about you being my stepmom 'cause I have a mom ... and Vi." With a quick look to Miss Amanda's alarmed face, Ginnie calmed herself and whispered. "But I wouldn't be mad about you being my stepmom."

"Your mom was good to you. Vi is as well." She patted the space next to her on the blue-and-white-checkered swing pad. "It's okay if you don't want me to be your stepmom."

"I didn't say that," Ginnie said quietly.

"What I meant was, this is a hard time for you. I've known you for a long time." She patted the swing again. Ginnie sat. "Until recently, you haven't seemed to miss your mom a whole lot and now that you are, you have a lot going on. Your dad told me about the scrapbook, and now I guess you have journals?" Miss Amanda waited for her to nod. "Todd won't let you read them?"

"No, and last night he said I could. That's why I'm so mad."

"That would make me mad too."

Ginnie stared at her, trying to remember the last time she'd seen Miss Amanda angry. Nothing came to mind. She tilted her head to the side. "Do you even get mad?"

"Yes, I just boil inside. I don't like other people to yell, so I try not to."

"That's like Daddy, the not yelling part, well usually he doesn't yell." Ginnie leaned back and giggled. "Today he yelled some. Usually he just shuts his mouth and glares. Uncle Ben does that, too."

A faint smile lit Miss Amanda's lips. "You did seem to be trying his patience."

Ginnie crossed her arms. "This time it's *his* fault."

"He knows that. Or he would have gotten mad when Toran stood up for you." Miss Amanda leaned closer until their foreheads touched. "I'm glad Toran stood up for you and I love that your dad listened to what he had to say. His love for each of his children shone through rather than his pride and anger. I respect that."

Ginnie let Miss Amanda's words soothe her.

"I don't think Toran's ever stood up to Daddy before."

"Not quite like that, but I remember you sassing your dad once and he sent you to your room to cool off. Toran looked at him and told Todd in no uncertain terms that you were his sister and he shouldn't be mean to you."

Ginnie felt her cheeks heat. "I don't remember."

"I do. Your dad told me later that from the time you two could walk, if he scolded one of you, the other would hug whoever was in trouble and say some version of 'she's just a little girl' or 'it's not nice to make my brother cry'. It used to make him crazy on one hand, but he liked that you stuck up for each other as well." Miss Amanda squeezed Ginnie's knee gently. "And sometimes your mom would take your side and then he'd have all three of you mad at him." She leaned back and sighed quietly. "She really loved you, Ginnie. She never wanted you to be unhappy."

"How do you know?"

"She told me."

54

SWINGING WITH MISS AMANDA

She told you?" Ginnie squeezed Miss Amanda's hand and wiggled closer. "You knew her?"

"Not as well as I would have liked, but yes, I met her a few times."

Ginnie tried to picture Mama in a real memory, but had to focus on one of the scrapbook photos instead. "What was she like?"

"Fun, happy, friendly. And really nice." Miss Amanda fidgeted with her watch. "The first time I met her I thought she'd be a snob, being how she was a nationally ranked beauty queen and all, but she wasn't. She was incredibly beautiful on the outside, but also on the inside."

Ginnie let Miss Amanda's words bathe her in a warm, cozy bathrobe sort of way. "Your parents really loved each other. I used to be jealous of them."

"Seriously?"

She nodded. "I was married to Jasper at the time. Of course I loved him, or thought I did, but then I met Uncle Ben and Aunt Sadie and knew what *real* love looked like. Todd and Queenie were like that. Whenever they looked at each other, there was definitely chemistry. She missed your dad when he went to work. Sometimes I couldn't wait for Jasper to leave."

Miss Amanda pushed the swing a little faster. "When you guys were about two-and-a-half, Jasper was talking with Uncle Ben. Your mom, Aunt Sadie, and I chatted here on the porch, watching you three play in the grass. Your dad drove up from work. Queenie jumped up and said, 'Excuse me, but I need to see my honey.' She ran to him and it was like watching a movie. He picked her up and twirled her, kissing and laughing with her. I wanted that."

Ginnie .widened her eyes.

Miss Amanda's cheeks pinked. "Not with your dad. Well, maybe *now*, but not then. I wanted Jasper and I to be that close. We were for a short while, but not like them." Miss Amanda wiped her hand on her black pencil skirt and sighed. "Then you and Toran joined them squealing, 'Daddy's home!' and the four of you hugged each other. Todd had you and Toran in either arm. You two wrestled to see who got to hug him first. It was such a sweet scene."

Ginnie rolled her eyes and smiled. "That's sounds kinda syrupy, but nice."

"It *was* syrupy ... *and* nice." Miss Amanda returned the smile. "I don't know if I could ever make him that happy, but I'd sure like to try."

The wistfulness of her tone made Ginnie pause. "You *already* make him happy. And I even told him that you should kick him to the curb 'cause he's boring. He just laughed and said he was glad I wasn't you. He likes you. He told me."

Miss Amanda's cheeks blushed a deep red. "I like him too."

"Why?" Ginnie grinned and then shook her head. "Don't take this wrong, but he's not cool. He's old-fashioned and kinda lame. Uncle Jake would be a lot more fun to be married to."

"Maybe, but I've liked your dad for a long time. Not that I don't like Jake, I do. Just in a big brother, friend, kind of way." She shook her head and gave a half-hearted laugh. "This is getting awkward. I just want you to know that if your dad and I do get married, I don't want to replace your mom. Nothing has to change between us. We can still be friends, like we've always been."

"So it's okay if I need to get to know my mom for a while?"

"Yes, and I'll see what I can do to help you."

"Like talk Daddy into giving me the journals?" Ginnie wiggled her eyebrows hopefully.

Miss Amanda laughed. "I'd love to say 'yes', but he seemed pretty determined to keep whatever secret he wants to keep. I've never seen him quite like this."

Ginnie tapped her chin. "I bet he tells *you* the secret." She sat up straight. "Will you tell me if he does?"

"I'm not sure I want to know. *Especially*, since you want to know so much." She shook her head. "If I know and don't tell you, it might cause problems."

"And if you find out and tell me, we could be best friends," Ginnie suggested with a grin.

"Nice try. Then Todd would never trust me again. I couldn't do that." She stood and held out her hand. "Are you okay?"

Ginnie took it. "Thanks for staying with me."

"Anytime." Miss Amanda hugged Ginnie tight. "You've been like my own for some time now. I'm glad you and Tillie are friends." She kissed the top of Ginnie's head. "I'm sorry Queenie isn't here. I know you love and miss her. Whatever you need me to be: friend, big sister, stepmom, I'm here for you, okay?"

"Okay." Ginnie took a step toward the door. "I'm going to read the journal Mama wrote for me again."

"Good idea. Should I tell Uncle Ben you need some space?"

Ginnie nodded. "And that I'll need to ride Calliope."

"Will do. Feel better." Miss Amanda smiled and waited for her to go inside.

Ginnie realized for the first time since she and Tillie dreamed up Operation: Secret Sisters, how she really felt about it.

Getting a step-mom might be just as cool as getting a sister.

55

LETTER FROM MAMA

Ginnie lay on her bed, eager to read the words Mama wrote to her, once again. She tried not to think about the journals she hadn't been allowed to read and fought the anger and sadness that welled when she thought of them.

Taking a breath, she cleared her mind and tried to remember the love and excitement she'd experienced last night as she read the letter Mama wrote to her for the very first time.

My Dearest Ginnie,

Welcome, Little One! You are here and oh, so perfect! I can hardly believe my eyes when I look at you and realize that the love Daddy and I have for each other created a perfect little angel straight from heaven. I have to pinch my arm to convince myself that you're not a dream. I've always wanted to be a mom and you and Toran (your twin brother) have made that dream come true.

I want to keep up with this journal, but I ask that you not hold it against me if I can't. I find it too hard to put you guys down long enough to write how much I love you. You and Toran are simply the two most adorable baby dolls that ever were. Watching you both grow is now my favorite past time.

First of all, let me tell you about your name. If you love it, thank your Daddy. If you hate it–tell HIM–it was all HIS idea. Your official name is: Virginia Maie Stratton West the second..

Your Daddy named you after me, Virginia Maie Stratton West. I grew up being called Ginnie, Princess, Widget, and other things that I don't want to admit to. 😴 Your Daddy wants to call YOU Ginnie. I did a lot of things as "Ginnie" and the name served me well.

Your dad has nicknamed me "Queenie" because he calls me the "Queen of his Heart"—corny I know, but sweet. So that's what I go by nowadays. Your Daddy's a little crazy, but a romantic at heart. Just don't tell him I told YOU so. 😴

At any rate, dearest Ginnie, we are so happy to have you in our lives. I have a lot of plans for you and your brother. You are lucky to be born into a farm family, because when you are old enough to ask for a pony, I will get you one. Or a Thoroughbred. I love to ride mine. Her name is Eternal Love.

I think we will start with miniature horses for each of you. I had one when I was young. Her name was Star Beam.

For now, I am content to count your fingers and toes and dress you up, my beautiful little dolly. I love to hear you breathe and when you sleep, sometimes you smile. I hope you always have pleasant dreams, my precious daughter. I can't believe I get to say that. "My daughter."

Nine months ago, you were a very good idea, a dream Daddy and I dared to wish. Today, you are here, a dream come true. Wests don't have baby girls, so I'm told. But I've always listened to the beat of a different drum and I'm glad we overcame the odds. Your daddy is especially happy. 😊

I always want to be here with you, because life is an awesome adventure. I think you know that already though. At only 3 days old, you aren't content to just sleep your days away. You're very alert. Life amuses you. You smile already and nobody's convincing me it's gas. I can tell you're like me. Maybe Daddy was right giving you my name.

Just promise me that you won't be as stubborn as me; I don't think that would be a good thing. One of me in a bad mood is enough. Your daddy is quieter. I think Toran is going to be like him. It'll be up to us to rock their world. 😊

I am sure the reason you two are so sweet is because your grand-mothers have been taking turns holding you in Heaven, before sending you on your way to Daddy and me.

I love you, my precious baby girl.

Love, Mama

Blinking, Ginnie tried to smile in spite of her sadness, pretty sure Mama would want her to be happy when she read this letter.

I wish you were here, Mama. It's kind of hard to 'rock' their world without you. Life's not feeling like an "awesome adventure" right now. It's feeling really hard.

She remembered Dad saying he was so sad when Mama died that it hurt to breathe. Wiping her eyes, she didn't even have to imagine how he felt. She knew *exactly* what he meant.

56

FAST AND FURIOUS

*G*innie leaned forward in the saddle and tapped Calliope with her heels, letting her troubled thoughts blow away as easily as the wind blew through her hair. The day had passed more quickly than she thought possible, given how badly it had started.

After losing herself in the journal from Mama, she, Tillie, and Toran splashed in the brook to beat the heat and humidity, skipping rocks and talking about the big secret.

"Maybe Mama was in the Witness Protection Program," Toran suggested. He picked up a pebble and made it skip five times before sinking.

Ginnie threw a pebble but it only bounced twice. "Could be, but what did she witness?"

"A robbery?" Tillie skimmed her fingers along the top of the knee deep water, and then sucked in a quick breath. "You don't think she saw a murder? That would be awful."

Toran shook his head. "She competed in horse events. Maybe she raced her horse and found out about some illegal betting or something."

"Could be." Ginnie picked up two flat pebbles. "It had better be something important like that, 'cause otherwise, when Daddy finally tells us, I'm gonna explode."

They tossed around other ideas such as Mama being a long lost heiress or princess around, but nothing made as much sense as the Witness Protection Program.

Uncle Ben didn't offer so much as one clue when he called them in for lunch. He refused to entertain their guesses. "Your dad said he'll tell you when he's ready. Leave it alone."

It was all Ginnie could do to keep her temper tethered. She was glad to wrestle with a few bales after mucking soiled straw from Calliope's stall. While concentrating on sore muscles, she didn't have time to think about Dad's betrayal.

Because they worked later than usual, Dad and Uncle Jake weren't home in time to help with afternoon chores.

As her frustration mounted, Uncle Ben's patience with her lessened. "Why don't you ride Calliope until you feel better?"

He didn't need to tell her twice.

Now she embraced the breeze. Calliope cantered effortlessly around the cornfield twice and then the alfalfa field for the third time. Ginnie slowed her to a walk for a final round, so she could put her mare in the stall for the night.

After taking off the saddle and putting it on its holder, Ginnie shampooed and rinsed Calliope off in the horse rack, then squeegeed most of the extra water from her back, and led her to her stall. She offered Calliope six slices of apple, giggling when Calliope's velvety lips tickled her palm.

She kissed Calliope's white forelock, then picked up her brush and smoothed the tangles from Calliope's mane.

"It feels good to get all the tangles out, huh, Calliope?"

Calliope snorted her agreement.

"So what do you think the big secret is? Mama's a long lost heiress or do you think she was in the Witness Protection Plan? Personally, I think the witness protection plan might work."

"Would you believe me if I told you that was the secret?"

Startled, Ginnie's gaze darted to the stall gate. Dad leaned on it, his expression wavering between amused and sad.

"Is it the truth?"

He shook his head. "No, but if it were, would you feel better?"

She shrugged and continued to brush her horse. "Are you going to tell me what the truth is?"

"I'm not going to tell you why I can't give you the journals back right away." Dad fidgeted with his wedding band. "I *am* going to ask you to trust me that I will *eventually* give them back."

Clamping her jaw shut to keep her protests corralled, Ginnie studied Dad's face.

His blue eyes bore through her. "I know that's not what you want to hear, but as your dad, it's my job to protect you. I take that job seriously." He opened the gate and walked in.

She squelched the urge to roll her eyes but couldn't keep the sarcasm out of her voice. "You make it sound like somebody will hurt me if I read Mama's journals."

"Let's just say that once you start reading them, you'll have a lot of questions. The real issue here is that I don't have a lot of answers for you. Your desire for answers will cause a lot of problems and hurt feelings. I just can't do that right now." He rubbed her cheek gently with his thumb. "I've never lied to you and I need you to trust me that I'm telling you the truth."

As much as she wanted to object, not one single, solitary exception popped into her head. She blew out a frustrated breath, trying to keep her tone civil. "Is it really *that* big of a deal?"

He nodded. "If it wasn't, I'd tell you."

Everything in her wanted to challenge his statement, but the sincerity of his tone kept her from speaking. Ginnie thought about a passage in the pink journal she had read earlier.

Mama had written:

I fear you have my temperament. "No" isn't a word we hear easily. I guess this is why you have two parents. I think your daddy will have an easier time dealing with you than me. He can usually talk me into his way of thinking.

Ginnie laughed.

"What's so funny?"

"Mama said in the journal that you can talk her into anything."

He chuckled. "I'd *really* like to know what she's referring to. She came up with some crazy plans, but they usually worked out well, so for the most part I just went along with her. We seldom argued. But we pretty much did whatever *she* wanted to do."

"Well, she said she's glad I have two parents 'cause I'm too much like her. But you told her you wanted me to be like her, so if I am, that's kind of *your* fault."

"You most definitely *are* like her." He stroked the length of Calliope's regal neck. "I was young and hopelessly in love. I didn't know any better when I wished that. But I figured out real fast that what attracted me to *her* sometimes scares me in *you*."

"Like what?"

"You're both fearless. You get an idea in your head and you just do it." He held his hand out for Calliope's brush. When Ginnie handed it over, he brushed the top of Calliope's back with long, firm strokes. "I didn't meet your mom until after she'd learned how to work around such nuisances as the law of gravity. So when she'd stand on Eternal Love's back, and prance around a parade ground and never fall, that was amazing." He stopped brushing and looked Ginnie in the eye. "On the other hand, when you jumped off the chicken coop with a blanket for a parachute, and ended up in the dirt with a broken wrist, that was just plain scary."

Ginnie rubbed her wrist and laughed. "It worked in a cartoon."

"Since your mom died of a broken neck, I'll take a broken arm any day. But my *preference* is to have you in one piece."

The reality of Mama's death hung over them like a rain cloud for a long moment.

Thinking back to Dad's reasons for not wanting to buy Tillie a horse and watching him slide Calliope's brush lovingly over her back, Ginnie thought how grateful she was to have Calliope at all.

Maybe I can give up trick riding for Daddy. At least I have my horse.

And I might be able to talk him into barrel racing eventually ... but I could give up trick riding.

She concentrated on his face.

He swallowed, blinking as he stroked Calliope's side. Several seconds passed. "I hated leaving you so miserable this morning. Amanda says you two had a nice talk."

"She's here?"

"She pulled up just after Jake and I did. I've been waiting for you to get back from your ride. Toran and I came to an understanding already. Now I want you and me to be okay."

"Me, too." She ran her hand gently down Calliope's neck. "I've been thinking about a lot of things today."

"Care to share?"

She turned to face him. "I want it to be okay to get to know Mama. And ..." Ginnie turned away and lowered her voice. "Does the secret make her a bad person?"

"Look at me, please."

She swiveled slowly toward him.

"You don't need to worry." He placed a firm hand on her shoulder. "Your mama was an incredible woman and you can be proud to call her your mother. She never did anything you need to be ashamed of." He handed her the brush. "Are you finished caring for Calliope?"

Ginnie nodded.

"Good, Uncle Ben has something to show us." He guided her to the gate. "I want you to be comfortable asking about your mom. I was eleven when my parents died and I remember a lot, but I still ask Uncle Ben about them." He opened the stall. "Oh, and you were right."

"About what?"

"About me being an ostrich. I have just ignored things I shouldn't, because it was easier." He closed the stall. "When your mama died, I was determined to keep her memory alive for you and your brother."

They reached the barn door and blinked against the early evening sun. "So why didn't you?"

"After she died, Toran would stand in front of her pictures and beg and cry for her ... like you did for Calliope a couple of years ago. We'd hold him and rock him, but he'd cry til he got sick or fell asleep exhausted. After a few days of that, we took her pictures down and he seemed to deal with her death better. I always thought I'd put them back up, but there was always a better reason not to. And then, being an ostrich about her just became the easiest way to go."

"That's really sad."

"It was. But now I am playing catch up and trying to balance your need to know your mom with my own conflicting feelings of loving her so much on the one hand and starting to have feelings for Amanda on the other." He stopped walking and faced her. "I suspect that's why you were okay with your scheme to get a sister, but blocked out the reality that your new sister would come with a new mom."

Ginnie frowned, protesting, "Miss Amanda said we could just be friends."

"And you can be, but she would still be your step-mom."

Hmmm. "Did you have a hard time letting Uncle Ben and Aunt Sadie become your new parents?"

"A little. Uncle Ben is who he is--is a good man. It doesn't matter whether he's really my uncle or my dad, he loves me and he's made sure I know that. Part of the reason I never wanted to marry again was I didn't think I'd find a woman to love my kids as much as their mother did, like Aunt Sadie did for me. But I think Amanda may be the exception."

Ginnie smiled, liking the idea. "So you want to marry her?"

"I think I do." He spoke in a cautious whisper.

She let his words repeat in her mind. A warm feeling grew as her understanding did.

She slipped her hand in his. "Would you want to, if Tillie and I didn't come up with OSS?"

"Probably, but it would have taken me longer to get around to it." He winked at her. "Being an ostrich about some things is still easier."

Ginnie giggled and followed him up the front porch steps into the farmhouse.

Dad led the way to the dining room, where Uncle Jake, Miss

Amanda, Toran, and Tillie sat at the dining room table looking at pictures.

"Check it out," Tillie called.

Toran laid pictures out in front of them. "Here's the three of us with Princess's kittens. And Uncle Ben--with Ginnie and Tillie."

"Very nice," Dad said.

Miss Amanda smiled. "I do believe these are the three cutest kids in the whole wide world, bar none."

"I was just thinking that." Dad winked at Miss Amanda. "Great minds think alike."

Tillie and Ginnie exchanged 'Oh, brother!' looks.

"While I agree, I think you might be even more interested in some other pictures that showed up when I looked through the memory card on Aunt Sadie's old camera." Uncle Ben pulled some photos from his shirt pocket. "These were the last pictures that Aunt Sadie ever took. I found her camera a few days ago. If you'll all bear with me for a few minutes, I think Aunt Sadie has a few things she'd like each of you to know."

Silence filled the room.

Uncle Ben smiled. "Todd, you told me you agreed with Toran that Queenie's journals felt like a letter from Heaven. And if a picture is worth a thousand words, I think Aunt Sadie has left a letter of her own ... for each of you."

57

LETTERS FROM HEAVEN

*U*ncle Ben motioned to the chairs.

Dad pulled out the one in front of him for Ginnie. She sat.

He stood behind her, his hands resting on the back of the chair. Uncle Jake winked at her from across the table.

Miss Amanda stood up from the end chair and walked over to stand next to Dad. She smiled at him and raised a questioning brow. He returned her smile. Both faced toward Uncle Ben when he started talking.

"Having had many conversations with several of you lately over the new changes in your lives and the paths you are considering, I've been pondering how to help you resolve your conflicting emotions." Uncle Ben took a second to look each of them in the eye. "And as happened so often when my sweetie was alive, she has given me the inspiration through these photos to help each of you find peace."

His gaze rested on Miss Amanda.

"Even me? I wasn't really a part of the family back then."

Uncle Ben chuckled. "That's what *you* think. In Sadie's mind, over time he became just as much her child as Jake and Todd. She loved him and tried so hard to help him. When he married you, you became a part of us as well. She had great hopes for the two of you. As did I."

"But Uncle Ben, you know what he did," Miss Amanda protested.

"I do know. I encouraged you to leave him when he hurt you and Tillie." He shook his head at Tillie when she opened her mouth to argue. "Loving him didn't excuse his bad behavior. And I certainly wouldn't ask you to stay in an unsafe situation. Aunt Sadie would agree. But she would still love him." When Tillie's mouth dropped further open, he continued. "Bear with me, please. You'll like where I'm going with this."

"Not if it has anything to do with *him*," Tillie groaned.

"Matilda Grace, don't be rude to Uncle Ben," Miss Amanda scolded. "Apologize."

An anxious quiet hovered for a few seconds.

Tillie glanced at Ginnie, who sat next to her, and offered an encouraging nod.

"I'm only sorry for being rude to Uncle Ben, *not* for being angry with Jasper."

"No one is telling you how to feel about Jasper. But I would ask you to *consider* that if you spent less time angry at him, you might be happier in your life all-around. He knows he was a problem for you. And he left, to solve that problem. He did that because he loves you."

Tillie shook her head and waved that notion away. "I don't *want* to love him. I don't *want* to like him. I just want him to *stay* gone." Her voice grew increasingly agitated as she spoke.

Ginnie tilted her head to look at Dad and grinned. "She sure could be my sister all right."

Uncle Ben leaned toward her across the table. "Understood. I'm not telling you how to feel about him. But the fact is, he's your dad. Dads love their kids, even when they aren't the best at showing it. How *you* feel about *him* is up to you. But *he* gets to love *you*—whether you like it or not. And since I know he does, I want that knowledge to help you, not hurt you."

Tillie looked like she didn't want to believe him, but Uncle Ben had on his 'patient' face and would wait for her to respond. She finally sighed when she realized everyone was looking at her. "Well, I still don't want to like him."

"That's your choice, but I promise you'll feel better if you quit holding a grudge." Uncle Ben fanned the photos in his hands like Mama had her fifty dollar bills and looked at Uncle Jake. "You two have been struggling on how to deal with Jasper—being's how Jake and Jasper used to be good friends, and then he made some bad choices."

"He hurt me and just left." Tillie stood quickly, making her chair fall over behind her. "That's not just a bad choice. That's mean and wrong."

Uncle Jake walked behind Tillie, picked up the chair, and placed a comforting hand on each of her shoulders. "Friendship only goes so far, Uncle Ben. I'm with Turtle on this one."

"I'm not making excuses for him, Jacob. I was just as appalled by his behavior as the two of you, but there was a time when *he* was the abused child needing us and try as I might to forget that, I can't." He cast a piercing look from Uncle Jake to Tillie, making Ginnie shiver a little. "But whatever his faults, Jasper loved Tillie and Amanda. I know that and so did Aunt Sadie."

Tillie jutted her chin. "Prove it."

"I thought you'd never ask." Uncle Ben placed two photos in front of her.

Ginnie giggled, surprised at Tillie's gumption at standing up to Uncle Ben. That was something even Ginnie didn't do. Dad seemed equally stunned ... and amused. He gave a quick shake of his head when Ginnie glanced at him.

She leaned in to see the pictures better.

Uncle Jake picked one up as Tillie took the other.

After a minute or so, Uncle Jake put his back down, grinning. "Leave it to Aunt Sadie to mess up a perfectly good grudge."

Ginnie picked up the picture. Uncle Jake and Jasper Taylor dwarfed Aunt Sadie, who stood between them with an arm around each man, hugging them tight. Each smiled as though everything was right in their world. Mr. Taylor held toddler Tillie lovingly in the arm that wasn't wrapped around Aunt Sadie. She leaned her head against her father's shoulder.

Tillie set down the picture she held. Ginnie picked it up. In it, young Tillie reached for Aunt Sadie from Mr. Taylor. Aunt Sadie's lips were puckered as though she were giving kisses.

"May I?" Dad took the photo from Ginnie and showed it to Miss Amanda. "I told you Aunt Sadie considered Tillie her other grandchild."

"Uncle Ben! That is so sweet!" Miss Amanda squealed. She waved the picture to Ginnie. "Do you remember when I was telling you about visiting with your mom? *This* was earlier that day."

"Where was I?" Dad asked.

"At work. Jake was home on leave. Queenie rode her horse and then visited with me and Aunt Sadie while Jake and Jasper caught up."

"These pictures might be of interest to the rest of you." Uncle Ben set several pictures quickly on the table, one at a time. Ginnie barely had time to register various photos of toddlers and adults before Toran snatched one close to him. "This is me and Mama."

Ginnie and Dad shared a grin and each plucked up a photo.

Dad held a picture of Mama and Miss Amanda hugging Aunt Sadie between them. Dad glanced from the photo to Miss Amanda, and then back again. He looked up toward the ceiling, then smiled, mouthing, "Thank you."

Ginnie wondered briefly who he was talking to as a peaceful feeling swept over her.

58

THE END

*T*illie jiggled Ginnie's elbow.

Ginnie turned to her friend.

Tillie whispered an excited squeal and pointed at Dad and Miss Amanda, who shared an extra-long kiss. Ginnie stared at them, a little surprised when they kept kissing, but very okay that they seemed happy.

"We did it! OSS worked!" Tillie whispered in Ginnie's ear.

Ginnie cupped her hand around Tillie's ear and lowered her voice. "It sure did. Daddy said he wants to marry her."

"E-e-e-e-e!" Tillie clamped her hand over her mouth and glanced at Dad and Miss Amanda.

Daddy wiggled his eyebrows while Miss Amanda giggled softly as they pulled away from each other. Tillie leaned next to Ginnie's ear and asked. "When did he say that?"

"When I was putting Calliope up."

"Awesome sauce!"

"*Totally* awesome sauce!" Ginnie turned her attention to the picture in her hand.

Mama was holding Tillie in her arms while Miss Amanda held Ginnie. She and Tillie reached for each other as their mothers smiled. She sucked in a quick breath and leaned toward Tillie again. "Check it out."

Tillie took the picture and gasped. "That's us. With our moms. *Together*." She held it up for Dad and Miss Amanda to see. "Look. We were best friends, even back when we were babies."

Ginnie smiled and reached for the photo. "Not just best friends, Tillie. *Sisters*."

~~~THE END~~~ (For Now)

AUTHOR'S NOTE: You can find out why Ginnie's dad took the journals in Book Three: Simply West of Heaven

AFTERWORD

A MESSAGE FROM
THE AUTHOR:

If you want personalized signed copies of any of my books, please visit my website:

http://TheHeroInsideMe.com

Or message me on Facebook: I'd love to be Facebook friends! You can find me at:

https://www.facebook.com/Author-Monique-Bucheger-193789017310198/

or Author Monique Bucheger on Facebook.com

I hope you have enjoyed reading this book as much as I have enjoyed writing it. Writing empowering and entertaining books has always been a dream for me, so I truly appreciate your support.

If you like my books, I would really appreciate it if you would leave a review at Goodreads.com, Amazon.com, Audible.com, Barnesandnoble.com, or anywhere else reviews are given, I'd love to hear from you.

It's easy and would help me immensely.

Just type my name in the search bar: Monique Bucheger, and all of my books will show up. Please write a sentence or two about why you liked it. You can copy and paste the same review to all places. This would really help me reach new readers.

Thank you. 😊 -Monique Bucheger

Resources for Child Abuse Help

Child Abuse Resources

National Coalition to Prevent Child Sexual Abuse and Exploitation: www.preventtogether.org

Prevent Child Abuse America
www.preventchildabuse.org

Healthy Families America
www.Healthyfamiliesamerica.org

Stop It Now!
www.stopitnow.org

Darkness to Light
www.d2l.org

Association for the Treatment of Sexual Abusers (ATSA)
www.atsa.com

Prevention Institute
www.preventioninstitute.org

Child Help USA

www.childhelp.org

Child Care Aware
www.childcareaware.org

The National Child Traumatic Stress Network
www.nctsn.org

National Children's Alliance
www.nationalchildrensalliance.org

Kempe Center for Prevention of Child Abuse and Neglect
www.kempe.org

International Society for Traumatic Stress Studies
https://istss.org

National Children's Advocacy Center
www.nationalcac.org

National Alliance of Children's Trust and Prevention Funds
www.ctfalliance.org

ABOUT THE AUTHOR

MONIQUE BUCHEGER

When Monique isn't writing, you can find her playing taxi driver to one or more of her 12 children, plotting her next novel, scrapbooking, or being the "Mamarazzi" at any number of child-oriented events. Even though she realizes there will never be enough hours in any given day, Monique tries very hard to enjoy the journey that is her life. She shares it with a terrific husband, her dozen children, one adorable granddaughter, two cats, and many real and imaginary friends. She is the author of several books and hopes to write many more. You can find more about Monique and her works at:

www.moniquebucheger.blogspot.com

A new website is being built at: http://TheHeroInsideMe.com

Downloadable free content will be available as soon as the website is live.

OTHER BOOKS BY MONIQUE BUCHEGER

Trouble Blows West: A Ginnie West Adventure

Putting her body in motion before her brain is in gear creates a mountain of problems for 12 year-old Ginnie West. She is certain that defending her twin brother, Toran, from the biggest bully in sixth grade was the right thing to do. But Ginnie couldn't be more wrong. She quickly learns that Toran doesn't appreciate being rescued by a girl any better than Pierce likes being knocked down by one.

When Pierce seeks revenge on Ginnie, Toran sets aside his anger and helps her plot a payback prank at Pierce's house. Sadly, Ginnie learns that Pierce has a reason for being a bully when she sees his dad drop him to the floor like a ragdoll. Realizing he's a boy in big trouble, Ginnie decides to be his ally, because he won't let her be his friend.

Simply West of Heaven: A Ginnie West Adventure

Twelve-year-old BFFs Ginnie and Tillie are matchmaking geniuses. Sweet! Not long after they schemed to get Ginnie's widowed dad to fall in love with Tillie's divorced mom, Ginnie stumbled upon her late mom's journals, making life even more awesome sauce ... until her dad confiscated the journals, determined to protect Ginnie from a danger he won't name.

Ginnie is counting on her future sister's help to make Dad change his mind, but Tillie's not so sure the ghost of Ginnie's mom will make a good addition to their new family tree. The girls' world gets flipped upside-down when a blast from the past shows up and makes Tillie go nutburgers. Ginnie is torn between helping her best friend and what could be the answer to her deepest wish.

Being West is Best: A Ginnie West Adventure

Twelve-year-old BFFs, Ginnie West and Tillie Taylor, are matchmaking geniuses. Together, they maneuvered Ginnie's widower-dad into proposing to Tillie's divorcee-mom. Sweet! Certain they are well on their way to sisterhood, each girl is floored when Tillie's lousy-excuse-for-a-father puts in an appearance after a six year absence. Too bad "lousy dad repellant" doesn't come in a can.

Even though Tillie's dad has sobered up and is determined to make amends, Tillie would rather he just disappear again. If he stays, "Operation: Secret Sisters" may need to be renamed "Operation: Not Gonna Happen."

If that's not bad enough, the biggest bully in seventh grade comes over often and wishes he could call the West's farmhouse "home." When the bully's abusive dad shows up as well, Ginnie thinks it's time to change her family's motto from "When you're here, you're family" to "There's no more room at the West's."

The Ginnie West Adventure Collection

Multi-Book set (Featuring Books 1-3)

Popcorn: A Picture book featuring Ginnie and Toran when they were 3 1/2 years old

When hunger wakes little Ginnie from her dreams she sets out to make herself a midnight snack. Hilarity and trouble ensues as she wrecks the kitchen in her attempts to make homemade popcorn balls.

For More Great Content

Including Free Downloads Visit:

https://TheHeroInsideMe.com

For more about about the illustrator,

Mikey Brooks, visit:

www.insidemikeysworld.com

Made in the USA
Columbia, SC
01 October 2022

68473166R00152